Nobody's Business

Also by Penelope Gilliatt

Nobody's Business

STORIES BY

Penelope Gilliatt

NEW YORK · THE VIKING PRESS

To Lillian Hellman

First published in 1972 by The Viking Press, Inc.
625 Madison Avenue, New York, N.Y. 10022

SBN 670–51497–7

Library of Congress catalog card number: 77–186943

Printed in U.S.A. by The Colonial Press Inc.

All the stories in this collection originally appeared in *The New Yorker*.

Contents

Nobody's Business

FRANK

➤➤➤-➤➤➤-➤➤➤ Matthew Paget, a cyberneticist at work on a
Family Robot Adapted to the Needs of Kinship (FRANK),
looked down from the eighteen-eighties Russian novel he was
reading to speak to the four-year-old daughter sitting under
his desk on his right foot. She was called Aston.

"Your mother sends you her love," he said.

"Where is it?" said Aston.

Matthew stomped out of the room, anxious not to weaken.
He cultivated grievance in the pantry for a few minutes. My
wife gallivanting in Rome. (She was working, in fact.) Leaving me to the devices of an enemy housekeeper. (Mrs. Trumbull, his ally.) He went back into his study, glaring on the
way at a prototype FRANK in the corner, which was plugged
in and idling like an electric typewriter with nothing to write.
He dismembered its initiative for the time being and sat down
at his desk again.

"Your mother may well be away for *months*," he said dra-
matically, although he knew she would be back next week.
"She has obviously deserted us. You and I will have to stick it
out as best we can." He sighed and joggled Aston with his
right foot, where she had resettled. "We can only hope she's
having a good holiday."

"She's working," said Aston.

"Humph," Matthew said, lonely.

"Ho," said the child, hearing that. There was a pause.

"Of course, I may become ill," Matthew went on. "Or you may. Who can tell?"

"I'll look after you," Aston said. "Can I show you my somersault? You're not watching."

"I have to go riding now," Matthew said, as if that were grim.

"Can I come?"

"I'm going with the rabbi. No."

The child did a handstand for relief, and Matthew went riding. A young Englishman teaching in a New Hampshire university, he had struck up a friendship with the local rabbi partly because they shared a style of high dudgeon. Matthew's was the fiercer, by a particle. He clung to it. He was eminent for it. Indeed, in this time of the politics of happiness, when people were privately much sobered, his friends and fellows looked to him for it, since the thundering held an energy that was at odds with the doom he alluded to. It was entirely cheering. The man overruled the matter. He did not know this of himself.

Cherishing rancor and pretending to champion the drab, he was actually a dashing man with a buried admiration for exuberance and mayhem. He had hopes, well hidden, that FRANK might suddenly develop boisterous tendencies. At the moment the robot struck him as rather craven. The prototype in his house could reply to typed messages, harmonize tunes, wave in answer to "Hello," and hold a conversation of a sort, drumming up self-assured remarks about the topics it had been rehearsed in. It could also trundle its way from room to room in answer to a properly put shout, negotiating a road through the imported English furniture by bumping cautiously into things and then backing away to try a forty-five-degree variant. The blind pains that it took were a triumph of programming. All the same, Matthew would have liked it better if it had shown some wildness; he was much interested by the machine's intellect but not by its temperament, which reminded him of his mother's. The elder Mrs. Paget also had a trudging nature, insuperably sunny and anxious to fit in. Whenever she stayed with them—with himself, his wife Molly, Aston, and the sceptical Mrs. Trumbull—there would be a closing of the ranks, and scorn for the alien pussyfoot in their midst would run through the house like flu.

Matthew had gone hacking today in fine black hunting boots and a beautiful purple stock. The rabbi got the quieter horse. They took this one by turns. The other was extremely nervous. Matthew looked at the rabbi, who was cantering contentedly, and shouted in envy, "That animal's moping!" His own petrified horse naturally bolted at once. Holding on by the reins, he yelled to the receding rabbi that this was the horse's natural gait. Much farther on, half a mile away and out of earshot, he said aloud that he was scared and called for his wife. ("She sends her love." "Where is it?") He crashed through branches, sawing at the horse's mouth, and then found a hill to aim the animal at in order to slow it down. He rode horses on the hypothesis that they answered the rules governing bicycles. The assumption generally worked, more or less. The horse was successfully braked today. It finished in a state of lathery obedience, with Matthew not fussed. All the same, when he came home, he told the rabbi and Mrs. Trumbull that he had been killed "as near as makes no matter," and there was somehow an implication that the peril to him continued even now. The rabbi ate some English biscuits calmly.

"The die is cast," Matthew said in Latin, stalking about the study.

The rabbi translated for Mrs. Trumbull.

"Not *again*," said Mrs. Trumbull. "And another thing. Mrs. Paget telephoned from Rome. While you were out. She said there wasn't any point in your trying to ring her back because she'd be out by the time you got through."

Overcome by what he had missed, Matthew sent the rabbi away and watched television with Aston. "This is the politics of happiness," he said, looking at the President's wave and teeth.

"Is he any good?" said Aston.

"What do you think?" said Matthew.

"Lousy?" said Aston, after looking.

"You might be right," said Matthew.

Then there was a newsreel film of a boy burning himself to death in protest against the war in Vietnam. Matthew turned off the switch just in time, and directed Aston's attention to the robot in the corner, and thought of the students in his classes who had gone to jail for defying the draft. Aston watched FRANK.

"Come to point D2 from point F by the shortest way, please," Matthew shouted to it in a level tone that was quite unlike the shout he used to the rabbi.

"He knows this room very well by now," Aston said, watching FRANK feeling a way to the fireplace. "He hasn't bust anything for ages."

The robot came to a stop by the mantelpiece and sang "Climb Every Mountain" from *The Sound of Music*.

"Oh lord," said Matthew. "Where did he get that from?"

"Professor Gregson taught it to him while you were riding."

"Shut up!" Matthew shouted to FRANK, and the song stopped.

There was a pause, and then the robot typed out a message:

"I have completed a sassy peregrination." Matthew held his head.

"What's the matter?" said Aston.

"The death of slang," said Matthew.

"It's not FRANK's fault," Aston said.

FRANK went on typing. "As of that time when I commenced the excursion, it was six thirty-five. At the present time, it is six thirty-eight and thirty-three seconds. Hopefully, I shall improve on this track record."

"Come to point B3," Matthew shouted.

FRANK buzzed and stayed still.

"Please," Matthew added, and FRANK trundled to him. Matthew typed a message on a control keyboard: "Strike out 'Hopefully, I shall improve on this track record.' Learn instead 'With any luck, I shall get better.'" He fed the message to the robot grimly.

"He was only trying to chat," Aston said.

FRANK whirred and waved a tin arm and typed out: "Now we have another topic on the griddle. Let's kick it around."

Pause.

"Why are you grumpy with him?" Aston said.

"My house is being turned into a gymnasium for gobbledygook," said Matthew, as if the robot had nothing to do with him. At the same time he tinkered with it tenderly. "Things are quite impossible enough as it is, with your mother gadding about like this and telephoning while I'm riding. Well, we shall have to push on, in the teeth of everyone, I suppose. Give FRANK a word. Anything in this room."

"Sofa," said Aston in a loud clear voice.

FRANK digested and typed. "Our sofa is soft," it wrote. "Is your sofa foreign?"

"That's a bit better," Matthew said fondly.

"Do you enjoy sofas of foreign origin? I have observed sofas from Chippendale and New Jersey," FRANK wrote.

"Isn't that an interesting mistake?" Matthew said. "Aston, do you know what the mistake was in that sentence?"

"Yes," Aston said. "New Jersey isn't foreign, it's here."

"Well, that's true, but it's foreign to FRANK. As far as FRANK's information goes, England is still home. It's one of the things I never reprogrammed. The mistake was classifying Chippendale as a place, like New Jersey. The Chippendales were a family who made furniture."

"Oh yes, I forgot. You told me that before," Aston said.

Matthew admired her memory, and then made a mouse for her out of his pocket handkerchief, folding it formally and getting it to jump up his coat sleeve by flicking it from behind with his middle finger. The trick came off stylishly.

"Do it again," Aston said.

"No!" he said, slumping. "I'm *exhausted*. None of you seem to realize. You wear me out, all of you."

Aston took no notice, as he wanted her not to. "What does the robot learn next?" she said.

"How'm I expected to work when there's this shambles to be put to rights?" he roared, glaring at the room, which was tidy.

"I'll do it," Aston said, looking round for anything to clear up and finding an ashtray with some of his pipe tobacco in it.

"The robots at the lab are better than this one," he said, watching her. "In a year or two they'll be tutors and secretaries and research assistants. You'll see. This one's more for company."

"He's not really much company," she said, though not wishing to wound.

"He will be soon," Matthew said. "Would you like to do an experiment?" He sat Aston under a black hood with a hole in it, and showed her a drawing, part by part, through the hole.

"What's this you can see now?" he said.

"A leg," Aston said, muffled under the hood. "A drawing of an animal's leg."

"What animal is it going to be?"

"Well, it might be a cow, it might be a zebra, it might be an elephant. Who drew it?"

"Me. I was disguising the style. O.K., that counts as one move. Now suppose you're only allowed one more move to tell what the animal is. What do you want to look at?"

"The head. It might be a man with peculiar legs, but I could tell that from the head, anyway."

Matthew took the hood off her excitably.

She said, "Oh good, it was an elephant."

He said, "It's brilliant." He strode quickly up and down the room with his hands in his pockets, skipping round the robot, whom he had set to tacking back and forth on the carpet.

"What's brilliant?" said Aston.

"The way you did that. FRANK still spends three moves counting legs to decide whether the drawing's a man or an animal before he asks himself what sort of animal. You went straight to the head in one, and you're not five years old yet."

Mrs. Trumbull came into the room and tried to sweep the child to bed.

"Don't take her away," Matthew said. "Please," he added, seeing mulishness and remembering the robot. "We were having a nice time. It needn't be bed quite yet, need it?"

Mrs. Trumbull suddenly burst into tears and stood with her head bent down onto the top of the marble mantelpiece. Matthew looked at her, feeling pity and panic, and gestured Aston out of the room. She went as far as the hall and looked back at him. He nodded, and she waited by the doorjamb. Mrs. Trumbull's shoulders shook. She dried her eyes with a Kleenex and threw it into the fire, where it hissed.

"What's the matter?" Matthew said, trembling. "Aren't you happy?" He looked at her strong back. "You're *always* all right!" he shouted at her. "You've never done this before. Are you homesick?"

She went on saying nothing and leaning her head against the mantelpiece.

"There was once a slave leader," Matthew said, "who led a rising in the West Indies, and he was shipped off to prison in France, a very cold prison, damp, where he taught himself to read, alone, and then taught himself French so that he could write to Napoleon to ask for his freedom. . . . He died standing up. He was propped against the wall. He seemed to have decided just to stand there. They found him with his forehead against the stone. I'd forgotten it. His *forehead*. . . . He must have died while he was *thinking*. . . . Against *stone*. . . ."

Pause. Mrs. Trumbull moved. "Thank you," she said.

Matthew took in again that Aston was standing by the door. "Could she have heard that?" he said in a low voice.

"Of course," said Mrs. Trumbull, still facing the fire. "But it wouldn't be the first mention of it. There was that kitten dying. She never did believe our tales. She sorted it out in her mind later."

" 'Strewth!" said Matthew, starting to back into anger. "There's never a day without some upset."

"You're not really a hard man, whatever they say," Mrs. Trumbull said.

Alarmed by her rare open fall into the giving of compliments, his mind fled. He remembered playing billiards in Paris one night. He got up, and put on his coat, and rasped that he was going to take her and Aston and the rabbi to shoot pool in the village.

"It's too late for Aston," Mrs. Trumbull said.

"Don't be stuffy," he said. "We can dress up. Aston can pretend to be a hippie. We'll take her on the horse. The *easy* horse," he added bitterly, the bitterness being for form's sake. "Not the one that nearly cost me my life."

He corralled the rabbi, and they went into the village. Mrs. Trumbull looked stoic again. Aston wore ropes of her mother's beads, a hippie scarf round her forehead, her father's riding gloves, and her own gum boots. She sat astride the horse while Matthew led it. The rabbi followed slowly in his Peugeot with Mrs. Trumbull. The car once came too near, and Aston swayed. Matthew caught her before turning round to bawl. "You were deliberately trying to run me down," he said. "Is there no *end* to it?"

"I can't listen to you for the moment. I'm in the middle of changing gears," the rabbi said. "I suppose you think it's easy, driving a non-automatic at this crawl." He put the car dolorously into first. No mean playing partner for Matthew, he could make even a need to change gears seem the blow of a fate hellbent on singling him out.

Mrs. Trumbull said, "I see you double-clutch. It's the mark of a generation." She smoothed her gloves.

Then Aston nearly fell off again, and whimpered, and Matthew vaulted up behind her. He moved her onto the horse's withers, where she felt magnificent. "Now *Aston's* getting in a state," he moaned to the trailing car, holding on to her, and she to him. "There's no consideration. She *knows* I can't stand her getting in a state." He carefully gave her the snaffle reins, which would do the horse's mouth no harm, and told her they might as well both hang on to the saddle.

Mrs. Trumbull looked at him for a while. "I wouldn't mind putting my slippers under his bed," she said to the rabbi.

"No good will come of this jaunt," said the rabbi.

Near the village they passed some Sorbonne students on an exchange year at Matthew's university. They were chatting and shouting to each other in bunches strung across the street.

"Is that Spanish?" Aston said.

"No, it's French. French is another language, just as Greek and Latin and Russian are other languages."

"What language does FRANK speak?"

"Nearly English, but partly maths. Robots don't quite speak English. There are other robots that speak things called Cobol and Fortran but they're fake languages. There are some kinds of words they haven't got. They can tell you you've drawn an elephant but they can't tell you whether they think it's a funny drawing or a rotten drawing. If we could ever get a robot to do that, we'd have done something new. It would be the first time."

Then it occurred to him that a four-year-old was constantly doing things for the first time, that Aston was riding a horse for the first time, and so there wouldn't be any reason for her to share that excitement, but she caught the note.

A troupe of twenty-year-olds sailed by on roller skates, blowing soap bubbles and weaving in and out of the people parking cars at the cinema.

Matthew and Aston shot pool. The rabbi and Mrs. Trumbull changed places with them later. Some of Matthew's graduate students were there. One was playing a guitar and singing his own love poetry in a corner. A physics major. Another was reading Allen Ginsberg aloud. It slowly seemed not the worst of times but a wild and hopeful year. Matthew sat for a while and listened. He pushed up his eyebrows with his fingers, one after the other, which was a habit he had, and thought of young men in St. Petersburg reading *The Possessed*, and talked to a scientist he liked. It was an evening that made him want to speak every language. "Books for Sale or Rent," a notice said in the main street of this village in the continent that was held not to be reading any longer. In my sere and unruled state, thought Matthew, without my wife, banging against the sides of strangers like a ship hitting a quay in the dark, the thing to do would be to write her a letter. It had best be a good letter. Though it will never get to her, the posts in Italy being what they are.

"When Mrs. Paget rang," he said to Mrs. Trumbull after they had gone home, "was there the usual echo on the line or was it all right?"

"You couldn't hear much," Mrs. Trumbull said. "She kept going off. I thought she was opening the door to a waiter. Several times I imagined her going to open the door to her dinner, but then she said she'd been there at the desk all along. Goodness knows what we lost."

"Idiots say that the problem is communication," Matthew shouted. "The problem is the *communications*."

"I daresay."

Matthew wrote a letter to his wife. It went badly, to his mind. Not my business, he muttered in his head, to have to produce this soup. What one says is usually a poor substitute for thought. And yet it's only when one says things that one feels a man, alive and kicking. He looked at the letter with the disgust that he reserved usually for minor ailments, and was in the act of tearing it up when he gave it to the robot to rewrite in its own way; thus:

GENTLEHEART,

You are my hungry fellow-feeling. My awe curiously cleaves to your footprints. My liking yearns for your spectacle. Aston and I travelled on the silent horse and played a game of skill with Mrs. Trumbull. The rabbi is a terrible

motorist. Please come back. You are my wistful sympathy.
I feel heavy-shouldered.

Yours,

M.

He kicked the robot, and then sat down and did some experiments. The effect of FRANK's company as they played draughts together unfortunately began to bring back the sprightly grownups who had come to see him when he had had measles as a child. They had played games with him by touch in the darkened room, speaking in bright voices and laboriously explaining the rules as if he had lost his wits. Tonight the robot started by winning, describing with the same intolerable cheer the strategy of its success, and then it annoyingly didn't change its tone when it began to lose. Matthew routed it three times in a row, galvanized, and prowled around the house to look at Aston, and eventually tore up both his own note and the robot's. There was something awry in the place, although he couldn't put his finger on it. It would have to do with the lateness of the hour, he said to himself. I can feel a wound somewhere in the house and I don't know if I delivered it. There's a scar somewhere and I don't even know if it's mine. We are supplanted as soon as we're born, that's the feeling. Deposed heirs, that's the feeling. No armies. He fleetingly saw his species in the grip of this innate sense, an old intimacy with dispossession that human beings seemed never quite to lose, although it had always been better known to literature than to politics or to his own science. He picked a few scraps of the robot's letter out of his wastepaper basket and decided to send the thing, pasting it together and meanwhile going over and over his thought, like FRANK tacking to and fro on the carpet. Well, we may be something after all. Unlike my goddam, happy, lickable horse. It's time we got out of Asia.

The telephone rang and he had a severe conversation with a

smug but scared colleague whom he suspected of plagiarizing the research done for a paper published by one of Matthew's assistants. At the same time as the row, he was wondering what it was that had made Mrs. Trumbull cry.

"You don't like me," the colleague ended up by saying. "You never liked me. If you spread this . . . this calumny, you'll be disliked by everyone."

"None of us is liked by everyone," Matthew said. "And some of us by fewer than others. Especially me."

He went into the kitchen to find Mrs. Trumbull, needing her company. She was drowsing in a rocking chair by the oven with a letter in her lap, which she put quickly into her apron pocket. She was looking troubled again, and he suddenly guessed that she must have had news that her husband in England was ill. A goose walked over his grave as he feared for his wife.

"Letter from England," she said, shaking her head and banging her left ear with the heel of her palm as though she had been swimming.

"Have you had a bad dream? Did I wake you?"

She looked at the letter sticking out of her pocket. "It's all strikes and Prince Charles in England, isn't it? The stamps used to make you think of home, and now they make you think of the cost of living."

"Your husband's not poorly?"

"He got a cold the day after his birthday, but then people often come down after a birthday, don't they."

"Wouldn't you like to go back sooner than the summer this year? It's been a good three months since you saw him." He paused, hating the opinion he was going to put next but making himself carry on. "You should pack it in with us. You could afford to stop by now. You've been working since you were twelve. With you abroad like this, he must feel as if he's married to a merchant seaman."

She avoided the point and started to steam the English stamps off the envelope because Aston collected them. "Well, I'm due for my pension, but it's nicer to keep working, isn't it? Anyway, I can't get the pension while Mr. Trumbull's still at his office, and he'll never leave. He's been there forty years. They must like him. Of course, he knows the files."

Matthew sat on the kitchen table and let her go on. Middle-of-the-night monologues. The present tense, used of someone away. He understood that.

"The Queen came round to his office the other week. He's doing something hush-hush. I'm sorry for the Queen, poor thing. Four or five changes of clothes a day, and always smiling, and always all the people she sees being so *old*. Those ambassadors. No chance of a bit of platonic friendship or a bit of fun, is there? All those old codgers. No chance of slipping away for a fling or a flatter."

"Shall we have some toast and marmalade?" Matthew said.

She made some under the broiler, which was more like the grill she was used to than the toaster was, and Matthew looked at the envelope, which was sticking out of her pocket again.

"Mr. Trumbull's a genius with the files. He remembers every paper that comes in and out. Ministry of Defence. I don't know much about it."

"Would you like to go back straightaway?" Matthew said.

No reply.

"I sometimes ask him, how can you stand it? I couldn't. All that fiddling about. He has to check the papers in and out, and then there's a security man who comes for him to hand over the keys. He knows every sacred thing in those files.

There's a lot of young chaps coming up but I don't think my husband likes them because he doesn't tell them much. They're in the dark. About two years ago with the spy scare the Ministry started checking up on us, in Wales even, with my family. Questions. What was my politics, all that. Who were our friends. Well, my husband's a terribly shy man and we don't have friends really, but they couldn't believe it. They even went to the dairy. The *dairy*. And asked things there. The woman that kept the shop took me aside one day and said a gentleman had been in, nosing about, and I said what was *he* doing, pray, and she said he asked if I had any debts. Going somewhere I'd been dealing for twelve years. Damned sauce. I felt like writing to them. I've never owed a penny in my life. . . . Well, as I say, my husband's a miracle for memory. He can figure income tax just like that."

She gave Matthew the jar of marmalade, avoiding his look, and sat down again by the range with her eyes closed. "He used to do the butcher's tax and sometimes the grocer's in the country, near where we kept a pub. He used to spend five or six afternoons and earn ten guineas. You've got to be an expert these days, haven't you? There's all sorts of little bits of money you can save yourself if you know how. Things you can put against the tax. . . . He always loved to absorb himself in things. He must know every piece of paper in the Ministry. Every high-up who hasn't sent some letter back at the end of the day. They have to sign for things they take out and they're not supposed to keep them overnight, you see. There are records written down, but he always knows who's doing it without even looking it up. Often he comes home and goes to bed at a quarter to seven after he's had his tea, and I sit downstairs and hear him swearing at those colonels as he drops off. 'Those bloody colonels,' he says."

"You miss him," Matthew said.

"Time enough," she said, opening her eyes and looking at him hard.

"Mrs. Paget would understand." He skipped a beat. "Hard to cope." (*Speaking for myself.*) "But you need a sight of him, woman."

"You've no call to be bossy," she said in the softest voice, watching.

"What's happened?"

Pause. Then, "I had a letter from Mrs. Paget," she said.

"You didn't tell me."

"She said she'd be away for a while."

"Not coming back next week?" The floor seemed to hurtle downward.

"I expect that was what she was phoning you about. I only got the letter after you went riding. It came special delivery. 'Express,' she wrote on it."

"Did she say why she had to stay away?" he said.

"She's tired."

"How bad?" he yelled. "Everyone keeps things from me."

"I couldn't say. She's thinking of being away until the summer."

"Where?"

"There was the address of a place somewhere."

"*Where?*"

She showed him his wife's letter, and the sight of her handwriting smote him. "I can't have an ill woman drooping about the house," he roared.

"She's just under the weather for a bit, I daresay," said Mrs. Trumbull.

"She *never* gets tired," Matthew said. "People belong together." He roamed the room and then said, "I'm sorry," for no obvious reason. None of us is liked by everyone, he repeated to himself.

He played with the robot most of the night. He telephoned Rome.

"What's this you wrote to Mrs. Trumbull?" he said to his wife. The connection was terrible.

"What, darling?" she said.

"What?" he said. He pushed on.

"I wrote to you a week ago," she said in the end, "to explain that I'd better have a holiday, but obviously you didn't get the letter."

He cursed blue murder, at one thing and another. "Suppose I get ill?" he said. "How ill are you?"

"What?" she said. "I didn't get anything after 'suppose.'"

"How ill are you?" he said, desperate.

"I've only got a temperature," she said.

"Help, it's not even Easter yet. How long do you need?"

"What? Perhaps if we try waiting a few seconds each time between speaking. I think the electronics get muddled if we talk over each other," she said, and he grinned at the very different intelligence of his wife, which had never conquered the concept even of a fuse but which still interested him more than anybody else's.

"I miss you," he said.

"I miss you," she said, but she was inaudible to him.

"What? I didn't get a word of that."

She started to laugh, and repeated herself loudly as the sound came back.

"Well, there's that," he said sombrely. "I thought you'd gone for good."

"What?" she said. "All I heard was 'there's that.' It's something you say, isn't it? Are you all right?"

"Given some things."

"What? The line went off again. I heard 'given,' " she said.

He snorted, pretending not to laugh, and said, "You won't be away long, will you?"

"What?" she said. "You'll have to yell."

"Take care of yourself," he said, refusing.

"What?"

"We should get out of Asia," he said.

"I'm not going to Asia. I'm going to Africa. Of course, you didn't get my letter."

"No," he said. "Take care of yourself."

"Could you hear about Africa?" she said, over him. "It's only because I need a break. I don't know why. I tried to write it. I love you very much."

"I'm hard on you. That's what you're really saying."

"What?"

"I love you," he yelled, and hung up, and felt an ass.

He spent the night working. He came into the kitchen early in the morning to make himself a thermos of coffee. Mrs. Trumbull was still there, making coffee for him herself. Her husband's letter was out of its envelope and lying beside the kettle. He did something that he had never done before in his life and read it, making a pretext to send her into the pantry for a muffin. Mr. Trumbull indeed badly needed his wife back. *But obviously she doesn't want to desert us. With my wife abroad. Help. . . . My wife. I drive them all away.*

"I'm afraid you must leave, Mrs. Trumbull," he said. "We should have someone local." At the same time he again did something quite against the habit of his nature, and put his arms around her and kissed her neck fiercely. "I don't know how *Mrs.* Paget's going to manage, of course," he said.

"She's depending on me to look after Aston," she said. "I couldn't go."

"Ah, but I spoke to her in the night and told her to come back at once. I can't have her away." This is my affair, he thought. Mr. Trumbull needs his wife. My wife needs leeway. People do what I say.

He bought Mrs. Trumbull an air ticket the next day and packed her off in a hurry, afraid that she might hear again from his wife with instructions about how to look after him. Mrs. Trumbull said she would be back in a trice.

"When is that?" said Aston.

"I'll be glad to taste some decent bacon again," Mrs. Trumbull said in a hard voice as he and Aston drove her to the airport. "Though I'll give you that the bottled mayonnaise in America can't be bettered. I'm sure I don't know how you'll manage. In fact, we could put off my going, couldn't we? Just until Mrs. Paget's home." She looked out of the window and wept at the idea of leaving him.

"Best done now," said Matthew. "You'll be back in the summer." They drew up at the sign for departures. "I can't stand airport farewells," he said. "I'm a busy man." He again put his arms around her, after Aston had climbed from the back seat into the one beside him, and then Mrs. Trumbull shook his hand and said, "We won't say goodbye, we'll say au revoir," except that she got it the wrong way round. "We won't say au revoir, we'll say goodbye."

Back at home, he put Aston to bed and arranged for a student to look after her, and waited for his wife's reply to the robot's letter, which would certainly come very soon. He fed FRANK some recognition problems. The robot did well. Matthew improved its system slightly. The robot did better. Matthew moved some of the furniture around.

"Come to point E from point G, please," Matthew shouted levelly, "and sing 'Green Sleeves,' beginning after collision two." FRANK blundered through the rearranged room. After the second careful bump, a Dresden vase toppled and broke. It was one that Matthew and his wife had always hated. The song began.

FRANK reported on the journey.

They went on working together.

FRANK deduced that not all dogs were spaniels, made a planetary calculation, rewrote a Yeats poem, and detected an undistributed middle in a syllogism.

Then, trying to engross himself in the news on television, Matthew spoke to the robot at a pitch it was not programmed to understand: "Have you anything to add?"

An Antique Love Story

➤➤➤➤➤➤➤➤➤ "The walls aren't vulnerable to dents," said the head of the office, leading a guided tour in a beautiful summer dusk. "What we have here is reinforced concrete." He led these tours each Thursday, after working hours.

Amy and I are a bit alike, thought a messenger boy called Ed. (His major work was the turning on and off of the lights every Thursday evening.) He looked at the people being shown round the modern office. The likeness may lie mostly in shutting up, he thought. What if she overrates me? I'm not in love with her. I never miss her when I'm not with her. (Though then he daydreamed of her in bed.)

"We think we have something quite new here in walls," said the head of the office, who had been talking all the while. He made a flourish at the concrete.

A visiting lady mayoress from England—Ed's country, and Amy's—found a nail file in her bag and tried to scratch the wall, and then took off her shoe and banged gaily with the heel. "Such a lot of walls now are pasteboard," she said to the office head. "These are concrete."

"Yes, these are reinforced concrete," the head of the office said. "We have something here that's not vulnerable to dents.

And this"—moving on—"is the main work area." Ed spent the day in the work area. He was twenty-four. There was cork on the floor and the ceiling. Everything—walls, floor, ceiling, desks—was in filing-cabinet gray. The machine that sold soft drinks and cakes was in filing-cabinet gray, with mushroom-beige panels and a design of stylized doughnuts.

"This *city*," said a businessman on the tour, slumping into a desk chair and talking to no one in particular. "I like living in New York, I tell you. Culture-wise, there's no city with half as much. Is there? Theatre-wise. Transportation-wise. Buildings. Restaurants. You can't do better any place in the world. Limousines. Who *cares* about the dirt?" But here he rubbed his hand through his hair and then looked at his fingers, which were filthy; and he shuddered at the three-day deposit of New York smog, and appeared resentful.

A tired section manager stared out of the window and bit his fingernails. "Yuh, it's the energy," he said. "On the go. I tell you, this office is like Grand Central Station when it's on the go." He gazed round the office, not savoring its emptiness after hours. There was a secondhand copy of Webster's International Dictionary open on a lectern. The architect had put it there as a last touch. Nobody ever looked anything up in it. It was the only old thing in the place. The secretaries had secretarial dictionaries to use if they ever needed them, but most of the girls were on computers. "I guess this place is beautiful when it's on the go," the section manager said.

"Well, it's a beautiful building," said the lady mayoress.

"Lived-in," said the section manager. He patted a counter gratefully. "These are a wonderful height. These counters."

"Insofar as our thinking is concerned," the head of the office said, "I believe I can say that our motivation, part of our motivation, is in the area of providing the work force with a work, er, area, that will meet their human needs."

A distinguished European visitor, a woman, mustered herself against him.

"We're watching now for results," the office head went on. "We've put a lot of thought into this. I'll be very interested to see how the work force responds."

Ed slipped away to his own desk and took a Kleenex out of the drawer. If I get rich, he thought, one of the first things I'll do will be to go back to linen handkerchiefs. It's the only thing I miss about the past, he thought firmly, although he was in the midst of peering around the office and hating it.

"The place we used to be in was pretty run-down, I'll tell you that," the head of the office said. "Now we've made this effort and we're beginning to see results. It was an effort, all right, but I'm happy to say it's paying off."

The troupe moved on. Ed turned on a farther set of lights and put out the ones behind.

"There's a gathering of strength," the office head went on to the visitors. The section manager, pleased, stopped biting his fingernails and then slouched exhaustedly into someone's desk chair. "There's a new vigor," said the office head.

"You'd have got the same effect if you'd cleaned up the old cloak-rooms," the distinguished European woman muttered. Ed heard her; he generally caught remarks that went by other people. A sort of fatuous cheerfulness seemed to him to govern most talkers, and he had an ear for the softly mutinous.

He wandered off, feeling underpaid and acutely hungry. He spent most of his wages on rent and wine and books. He often found and ate whole delicatessen meals thrown away in the office rubbish baskets. The amount of usable garbage in New York astonished him. Later this evening, for instance, when the tour party had left, he salvaged a perfectly good cold hamburger out of the wastebasket of a secretary he liked. The act quite cheered him, though the food was a little disgusting.

He rang Amy up. They began with their own silence. After some time, Amy said, "Hang on while I get a cigarette."

Wait until she comes back. There she is. Warm pause— what else? Wait again. What are we? Fond. Yes.

"It's nice you rang up," Amy said.

"Yes."

Pause.

"I don't want to talk about my life and I don't want to make small talk," he said. Pause. "Any more than you do." Pause. "As you know."

Pause.

"Is it hard on you?" he said.

Pause.

"What?" said Amy.

"Me not talking?"

After a longer pause, she laughed and said, "What are you blathering about?"

When he got home he found her washing her hair. It hung usually in a plait that was long enough to sit on. They tried to go to sleep later among the damp strands, which spread everywhere. She woke in the middle of the night several times, spluttering because she had hair in her mouth. At four o'clock she got up. "It's like the Sargasso Sea," she said, plaiting. "It's like going to sleep in weeds." Ed watched her. She came back to bed and hung the damp plait carefully over the side of the bed. "I should have done that before," she said.

"I'm hungry," he said. "I like your plait."

"What about some cold toad-in-the-hole?" she said.

"It's nice now," he said half an hour later. "It wasn't a good evening early on."

They had their silence, and then she said, "I think happy may really mean interested."

"People mostly seem to keep *pretending* to be interested," he said.

"That's what's been bothering you."

"Or else there's nothing there at all and they have to invent something," he said. "Everyone's talking to himself. Was it ever like this before? What are you thinking about?"

"That. Oh, and also not being keen on what I look like. I can see myself from here. It doesn't matter."

"You're beautiful."

"Perhaps I should try a fringe. Would you mind?"

"Up to you. Don't spoil your face, that's all."

She looked at him curiously. "What does my face consist of?"

They lived in a poor part of New York. Politicians called it "disadvantaged." They had two rooms. A child named Izolska lived down the hall. She had a Polish-Jewish father, recently widowed, who drove a taxi. The child spent most of every day on the floor above, with a retired old actress named Mrs. Green, because there was no school in the neighborhood for her to go to. She took lessons over the push-button telephone in Ed's and Amy's flat while they were at work. The scheme was called Touch-Tone-Tuition. It made the child fly back upstairs for company once a lesson was over. So long as Mrs. Green was alone with Izolska, she would watch her intimately and now and then give her dried pieces of fruitcake out of a big tin with Roosevelt's portrait on it, though anyone else's presence would often make her take cover in senile imaginings and refer to herself in the third person as Astrid-Agnes, after two sisters in a story she had read long ago. At other moments of threat she would say that she was God, knitting angrily and fending off questions.

On Friday, when Amy had left for work, Ed thought of throwing in his job to get on with something better. He looked at the telephone, and at the papers and library books on his desk (three planks on two trestles), and contemplated ringing up to offer himself full time to an amnesty movement he had once helped. And then he sheered away from commitment, and went to see Mrs. Green instead. Her knitting lay beside her, and she was talking to Izolska.

"Why aren't you at work?" Izolska said to Ed.

"Isn't it time for your arithmetic lesson?" Ed countered.

"Lessons on the telephone! They call that modern!" Mrs. Green shouted, reaching out to get her knitting for fear she would need it, but holding the child by the skirt with her other hand.

"I just thought I wouldn't go to work today," Ed said.

"You'll be fired," said Izolska.

"Well," said Ed, "yes." He looked at Mrs. Green, whose hand was still clutching Izolska's skirt. "Would you like her to have the lesson here?" he said to the old lady, seeing her dread of departures.

"She doesn't have a *telephone*, Ed," the child said. She contemplated adult blunders. "You two have the only one in the house, except Louie's, and his place smells."

"I forgot. Hadn't we better be going? Isn't it time?" Ed said to Izolska.

Mrs. Green started knitting.

"Not till eleven. You know, you don't have to sit with me," Izolska said. "I can use the door key fine on my own. I've done it lots of times."

"I'd like to hear the lesson. I never have," Ed said. Izolska looked at her Pop Art watch, which her father had given her last year on her eighth birthday. Mrs. Green knitted more intensely.

"What are you knitting, Mrs. Green?" Ed said.

Mrs. Green lifted the needles, working the while, and made the sign of the cross over him with them.

"What are you knitting, Lord?" he said.

"Human organs. Essential organs."

"I should think Izolska will come back here after the lesson," Ed said.

"Hearts, lungs, wombs," she said, keeping her eyes on the needles and not raising them as Izolska left.

Ed offered the little girl a Coke in his apartment, but she refused it and sat beside the telephone in a way that made him feel he should go into the other room. He lay on the bed and smoked. She put a piece of paper and pencil beside the telephone and doodled something, and then looked at her watch and sat still for five minutes, checking her watch several times before she punched the number of the Touch-Tone-Tuition office, which had given her an appointment with a computer. The telephone voice must have told her she had done something wrong, for she put the receiver down fast and then the telephone rang her back. She punched an identification number and was put through to the computer. The computer asked a question in a voice that Ed could hear. Izolska punched 1-5-6 on the telephone.

"Correct," said the computer after an eerie halt, going straight on to its next problem. When she was right, the computer would ask another question within one second. She was right consecutively for three and a half minutes. Then she began being wrong. When she was wrong, the computer was programmed to repeat the question. If she gave the wrong answer again, it told her the right one and went on to a new problem. This happened five times. Izolska started holding her hand against her left ear, although there was no noise in the room. After she had put down the telephone she shook like a little dog for a second. She asked for a Coke.

Ed got one out of the cupboard. Amy kept food there because it was the coldest place in the apartment. "It doesn't look much fun," he said. "It looks hard."

"The computer can't explain, you see," she said.

He asked her if she wanted to tell him the questions that had stumped her, hoping to help her, but she was learning the New Math, and his own old way of working out the answers only confused her. So then they had a game of two-handed poker, which cheered her up. She left politely after a while, and went to play with a ball against the wall with some other children in the street.

He lay in a chair to read, and remembered her on the telephone, and then he thought about Amy and himself. I don't miss her. I don't want to marry her. I never think about her when I'm alone, he thought, thinking about her. I don't give her much. I behave like some forebear of the robot. (*Help. Mustn't.*) I can throw up my job just like that. There's always something else. I could lose Amy, if I had to. (Unhappy.) A little read would be reviving, in the circumstances. He lay on his back. After an hour he jerked out of the book like a stranded fish, and struggled, and thought again of Izolska's hand against her ear on the telephone to the computer, and then of Amy and of whether he was behaving like a computer to her. He took the subway to the office where Amy worked and then circled the block, telling himself that he hadn't particularly got her in mind. Then he bought two paperbacks and went into a cafeteria for coffee, and Amy was there, at the head of the queue. He watched her with her tray. She had bought only a cup of tea. He saw her eye the tables and make for one that had a lot of food left on it, with no waitress close enough to clear the plates away before she had commandeered them. Living on leftovers was something he understood, but he had always thought himself alone in that economy. It struck him to the bone to see Amy heading for an uneaten roll and half a piece of pie.

He reached the end of the queue and put his tray down onto another table, standing with the cup of coffee in his hand and wondering what to do. She was wearing her plait down her back today. She ate from the two plates briefly and then pushed them away and looked for something in her bag. A dime. She made for a phone booth. He came up behind her and tapped her on the shoulder, and she spun round and said, "I was just going to telephone you." They sat down together and enjoyed themselves, barely talking. They went home later on a bus together.

"Something happened to you today," Amy said.

"Yes," he said.

"But we don't have to have a conversation," she said.

The man on Amy's other side, a middle-aged man with ragged hair and an interested face, prodded her knee with the end of the rolled-up New York *Post*, just as Ed was looking at her and saying, "Thank heaven for you."

"There's no doubt, of course, that the soul is female," the stranger said.

"Shut up," Ed said softly.

"The soul is female. One goes to it for advice," said the stranger. He fixed Amy with a wild stare.

"Do you?" she asked him.

"I shall dream about you, and my unconscious will decide what I think of you," he said. "It may decide you haven't been listening to a word I've been saying. It may decide I want to have an affair with you. Do you believe in reincarnation? I am related to earlier kings of the English and the French. This is why I speak with an English accent. I can tell you are both English. You notice I don't say 'British.' I believe the fact of the French incarnations to be the reason for my collecting of French furniture. When funds allow."

Ed took Amy's bag and looked inside it, needing something to do. The man rumpled his hair forward with his hand and said, "I'm afraid I'm a man who often bores people. I don't notice it. You must meet my wife."

"Yes," Ed said.

"Do you live together?" the man asked, following them to the exit of the bus. He put his foot between the closing doors so as to hear their answer, and the driver shouted at him.

"Yes," said Ed.

Amy stayed up late reading Simenon, and turned on the portable TV that Ed had borrowed. The news wasn't very good to hear. Then she looked at a movie with Humphrey Bogart, and filled in a form for a visa. She was planning a trip home to Europe. Ed was lying awake in the bedroom and he watched her for a couple of hours. After a time he saw her stomping around with her hands in the pockets of her jeans and a cigarette hanging out of her mouth, and he understood that she must be practicing a Bogey slouch.

By three in the morning she was in bed asleep and Ed still awake. He got up to take some aspirin and one stuck in his windpipe. The pain reminded him of being a child and of swallowing boiled sweets that he had tucked into his cheek to try to spin them out. Choking, he wondered whether he would die, and balked at that, and choked some more, holding the table and idly reading Amy's visa form through the coughing fit. She had broken off at the question "In the case of injury or death, whom should the authorities inform?" The name she had started to give, stopping halfway through the address, was her own. Moved, he paced the apartment. It was a warm night. At six o'clock, when he had finished his book and taken to trying to sleep on the floor so as not to wake Amy up—*programming* himself to sleep, he put it to himself, because wakefulness was clearly unfunctional and not fitting to the nature he thought he had—there was a knock at the door. There stood Bill, an old latcher-on who suffered twinges of paranoia late at night and roamed the city for acquaintances to attack with his insomnia.

"I knew you'd be up," Bill said, flying in the face of the evidence of bedclothes on the floor and an Ed barely dressed. They sat for a time. Ed could think of nothing to say, and of even less reason than usual to try. It seemed to him that he had lately been hearing many sorely awry efforts to talk. "Would you like a drink?" he managed at last.

"I knew you'd be up," Bill said again, glaring, and coming over to bore a finger into Ed's chest. "See here. I've something to say to you, buddy."

"Buddy?" said Ed. I scarcely know the man, he thought.

"I've something to say to you," Bill said. The finger pressed. "My nature doesn't allow me to conceal from you my opinion that you've behaved like a bastard to me. A bastard."

"What?"

"I came up here specially to see you, right? And yet you've deliberately never come to see me. What's more, you didn't ask me here."

"No," Ed said mildly.

"You admit it."

"Well, I'm very sorry, old boy, but I didn't mean anything by it." Ed concentrated uninterruptedly on the way Bill was now standing. He had his hand in his right pocket. Ed realized that he had a revolver in there.

"All I am to you is an acquaintance," Bill said, in the most alarming voice. "You make that clear enough. You treat me the way the British treated the Indians they did business with. Did they ever ask them into their homes? Not on your life. You bet. That's what I mean."

"But we *are* acquaintances. We hardly know each other."

Bill laughed bitterly. "That's just what I mean," he said.

Ed was invaded by holy calm and started counting on his fingers the possible number of hours' sleep left to him, given the good luck that Bill lost interest in murdering him and sloped off.

"Some friend," Bill said, helping himself to a drink.

Ed counted hours of sleep again.

"What are you doing?" Bill said, in a voice sharp as ice.

"Counting," said Ed.

"Counting what?"

Ed saw the physical provocation in replying "Hours of sleep," and said nothing.

"Counting what?" The revolver inside the pocket was pointing at him.

"Practicing scales, actually. Playing the piano," Ed said in hope.

Bill glared, and startlingly dozed. There is some mercy, Ed thought.

Next morning, Saturday, Ed woke at half past eleven and found himself alone and alive with Amy, who was laughing.

"Do you know what I did?" she said, giving him a cup of coffee. "I was filling in a form and started writing down me as the person to get in touch with if I was dead."

"I saw," he said, touching her nose. "It made me sad at the time."

"No, it's funny."

"Did you know that I nearly died last night? Bill blundered in at six in the morning, and he had a revolver in his pocket that he was going to use on me because he hadn't been asked to come. People do odd things on Friday nights."

Ed thought of himself as a man with no gift for weekends. It was part of his robot vision. He believed that, with luck, he knew how to use his own spare time functionally, but other people's seemed too much to dispose of well. Other people reposed too much trust. Other people wanted to go on outings and picnics that he might easily bungle. Other people tried so hard to believe that weekends were bound to be better than their weeks had been. Who were these other people, though? That morning, he thought with hatred of families sitting in cars bang on the verges of the summer highways, eating picnics to the roar of cars exactly like their own, but then he decided that these probably weren't the people he meant, to be fair. Now entertaining no great sense of superiority to anyone, he borrowed a car and drove Mrs. Green and Izolska and Amy to the country. With the gathering of the four of them life growingly seemed gay and splendid, although the age managed to put its oar in. Amy had to get out of the car to telephone the airline about her booking. They stopped at a garage. Ed listened in the booth.

"I want to confirm a reservation," she said. She gave her name. She had to plug her left ear, like Izolska, against the noise of the traffic.

"Sorry, Ma'am, but our computers are in malfunction."

"What?"

"You'll have to call again. We are unable to confirm your reservations at this time."

"Can't say either yes or no?"

"That understanding is correct, Ma'am."

"When shall I telephone again, then?"

"If you'll call again in one hour to one and one-half hours, our computers will be glad to speak with you."

In the car, Ed held the end of Amy's plait as he drove. Izolska sat between them. Mrs. Green, in the back, had brought with her a tapestry cushion cover that she was making. Amy turned round in the car and leaned her chin on the seat, like a tall dog propping its jawbone on the edge of a bed. Izolska hummed. They found a river and had a picnic beside it. Silence and interest gradually merged into a formidable hope in Ed's head, and he felt he had a bead on his life. Clicking a bottle against his teeth, he watched Mrs. Green listening to the news on the car radio. The car was parked thirty feet from where they were sitting. Mrs. Green sat on the front passenger seat with the door open, her feet on the ground and her head down, listening. She troubled over events in the world and had no trust in the President. She came back without words, and started to work furiously on her tapestry cushion.

"We all have these thoughts sometimes," Ed said, in reply to the revolt in her head.

Amy asked what the President had said.

Mrs. Green stitched. Izolska jumped into the river, holding her nose. "There are some human beings who do not wish for immortality at all," said Mrs. Green.

Amy swore at the President.

"No, we have to put up with the fact that people will always say and do things we find unforgivably disappointing," said Mrs. Green. "Do you care for this blue, or not? At the same time we have to preserve enough of the sense of outrage to change things. Are you two short of the sense of outrage?"

"No," Ed said.

"Only on Saturdays," said Amy.

"I wish you weren't going away," he said to her.

"It's only for a few weeks."

"Away?" said Mrs. Green.

"Amy's going home to England, and then she wants to go to Czechoslovakia."

"You'll be back soon." Mrs. Green opened her eyes wider as she said this and stitched hard at the tapestry.

"In a few weeks."

Mrs. Green here closed her eyes and said, "Leaving us."

"No, I'll be back. I live here now. Does anyone want a rest? Are you tired?"

"I don't want a rest. I've never liked rests. What a pity the longest day's gone. I always enjoy that. Still, October can be crackerjack. Look at that, now. Just enough of the green wool to finish. Well done. The week will yet be a success."

A butterfly came near, attracted by the colors of the tapestry. Ed held Amy's hand.

"You may be leaving him for too long," Mrs. Green said. "Although Czechoslovakia's an interesting place."

"Did you ever act there?" Ed said. "When did you give up the stage? I'm definitely—Amy, I'm definitely going to chuck it at the office. So I shan't be making much money. Will you support us?"

"Thank you," she said. "Thank you for asking."

"I'm not very good at that," he said, looking at her for a while and then turning. "Mrs. Green, sorry—I was interested —Czechoslovakia. Did you ever act there?"

"It's not easy, asking," Amy said to Ed, and then to Mrs. Green, "After Vienna?"

"I was told at fifty that I should stop," Mrs. Green said. "That was in London after the tour. They said I was in my prime. They thought I should end it there. Well, there were character parts I'd have liked to play, but one night I decided they were probably right. It wouldn't have done. I realized it the night I had to put on my glasses to see to cut up my meat." She paused. "It was on my birthday. There was a splendid party. You could call that a tonic event."

There was a congenial silence.

"You know I've only got one eye left now," Mrs. Green said.

Ed said "Sh-h-h" to Izolska, who was splashing them.

"Did I wet you?" Izolska said.

"Nearly," Ed said.

"There are people who don't like me, now that no one knows what I was. I can understand that. Still, I don't worry," said Mrs. Green.

Amy said, "Some people have an instinct ahead. Ed has. You have. Other people have an instinct behind. And then there are others who are exactly in step, and they'll obviously always be the ones who get on. They hardly have to open their mouths before everyone recognizes his own thoughts."

Mrs. Green packed up her tapestry. She had not talked of herself as Astrid-Agnes or as God all day. She crossed her legs and formed her fingers into a telescope and put them to her seeing eye, squinting at a tree.

"I lost my eye, you see, and that's why I don't have a television. I like the radio. Watching television is like having an electric current put through the good eye, and that's no help, is it? The authorities would give me a television set for nothing, but I can't stand it because it makes this good eye tremble, and that's no help to anyone, is it? As I said before."

Izolska watched the butterfly. "It likes the colors of my wool," Mrs. Green said.

Izolska started splashing again and sang a loud song to an out-of-tune yell of her own. "My pretty, pretty butterfly, come over here, it's Saturday," she howled, raising her head like a street singer baying at the sky in front of a cinema queue. I like it here, thought Amy. I like it here, thought Ed. The beloved child should be quiet, thought Mrs. Green. "*Basta*," the child told herself, out loud.

"Well," said Mrs. Green, "I'm afraid you've known me in the lesser years. It's time that does it. However, today sees me revived."

Ed took Amy away by the river and said, with his hand around her neck, "Would you be back for good, possibly?"

Staying in Bed

➤➤➤➤➤➤➤➤➤ "We have always been a very tired family," Finch said loftily to Henry, both aged twenty-eight, Finch lying back in a large bed with his cello on his ex-girl friend's pillow and Henry standing up by the gas fire. Finch was one of the most famous cellists in Europe, and Henry was known to a few as his accompanist. Finch pulled the bedclothes over his nose.

"You should get up more," said Henry. "I mean, you should get up at *all*. You've been there for over a month."

"I take furtive strolls to the fridge."

"You're too young to vegetate."

"I'm not young. I told you, tiredness runs in the family. Would you mind pulling down the blinds? The sun hurts my eyes." Finch turned on his side with an upheaval that he hoped to look final.

"What do you mean, tiredness runs in your family? When I've known you all since kindergarten and any one of you can wear me out?"

"My Aunt Belle was confined to her bed for many years," Finch said, blowing his nose in his health. He hummed something from a Beethoven cello sonata.

Henry hummed the piano part without thinking and then

41

stopped himself because he had meant to argue. "Hell, old Belle was always beetling around," he said.

"You know I hate inner rhymes," Finch said faintly, eyes closed.

"Your Aunt Belle never stopped going until she fell off the mule. How old was she in Tibet? Eighty?"

"Only seventy-eight," Finch said. "Anyway, that isn't the point. She always felt secretly whacked. All her life. She really always wanted to stay in bed."

"She went to prison seven times to get the vote, and she went to Ethiopia and Nuristan and the back of beyond on a mule, and you tell me she was always whacked?"

"It wasn't obvious to the naked eye, but we could tell. The family." Finch covered his head with the bedclothes and fingered some double-stopping on the mattress. He heard Henry's voice through the blankets. It was like the sound of someone blowing through a piece of pipe. They had done that together as children in the north of England, experimenting with different lengths of pipe.

"You're practicing," Henry was saying.

"Who said?"

"I can tell because you're humming. You've no idea of the racket you make when we're recording. I don't understand how anyone so musical can hum so out of tune with himself. You don't seem to be listening to yourself."

"I'm probably listening to you," Finch said happily. He came out of the bedclothes and said, "While I'm laid up like this, why don't you do a few concerts on your own?"

"It's not right, lying in bed all the time at twenty-eight," said Henry. It's not like him, he thought, contemplating their long life together and their long history of loving each other's girls. He was married at the moment, Finch not. They had a great passion for women, a great passion for each other, a great passion for music and trains. They would go on long train journeys together. In America, where they often performed, the trains struck them as poignant chiefly because uncared for, but they had found a friend with a long New England face who was a fireman on the run to Boston, and his professionalism and high interest in the topic of transport were entirely cheering. The trains in India and in Morocco had impressed them on recital tours as some of the most distinctive they had ever seen. Finch especially had the English love for nineteenth-century public transport. Ships, trains, buses, trams. Those elegant and ingenious objects of use. He and Henry had been going all their grown-up lives to the British Transport Museum in Clapham, running their fingers over the polished wheels, regretting the end of brass fitments, and taking in the beauty of the fish-net luggage racks. Finch had grown up in Northumberland, twenty miles from Henry, near the Roman Wall. Work had brought them to London, which they regarded as Down South. Anywhere in England south of Durham was still Down South to them. What Southerners called the North—Yorkshire, Lancashire—they called the Midlands, meaning scorn.

"You're a Celt," Henry said, brusque to his friend. "You're a born gate-vaulter. You shouldn't lie about in bed. You're not ill."

"Of course I'm not ill. I'm just tired."

"You should go to an analyst."

"An *analyst?* You've been brainwashed."

"It's unruly of you."

"To stay in bed?"

"The agents are going crackers about it."

"In the eyes of anyone who has noticed history, unruliness is

a great virtue in mankind. Would you like this pear?" Finch
lobbed it at Henry and then lay back.

Good throw if he's that tired, Henry thought, suspecting
something, but not finding it.

"I lugged that pear from the kitchen in the small hours,"
Finch said in a remote voice.

Henry wondered if his chum, the great young cellist, had
taken untimely to bed because he was trying to keep out of
Henry's marriage, or perhaps because he was nursing loneli-
ness. He had no idea that Finch was trying to get him to stop
being an accompanist and to work on his own.

"You don't exactly *lug* a pear," Henry said, eating it gratefully.

"You didn't say please," said Finch.

"It seemed a waste of time."

"No, it wasn't. Try it."

"Please," said Henry.

"Thank you," said Finch.

"Not at all," said Henry.

"Quite a bit," said Finch, suddenly perked up by throwing
the rhythm out and hoping that Henry would follow him because he wanted to see how it worked in canon. "Please," he
said.

"Thank you," said Henry, getting it.

"Not at all," said Finch.

"Quite a bit," said Henry perfectly.

"I think I may have a doze," Finch said, closing his eyes in
thanks. "Ring the agent and do the Ohio concert on your
own." He meant to look forbidding, but found it difficult when
eyes that should be glaring were shut. "You owe it to me and
to Betty. Your wife."

There was a long silence. "What are you actually thinking
about?" Henry said.

"About my father," said Finch. "And that I have had to get through a lot of long silences with both of you."

"If memory serves—" said Henry.

"It doesn't. It rules," said Finch. "Go and practice."

Finch was a lanky man whose cello made him look even thinner. He had a peculiar droning voice that reminded people of summer days and of buzzing from high up. It was often imitated, even to his face, but he paid no heed whatever. He had a copious nature with a touch of riot in it. Henry liked his company because it was convivial; the staying in bed disconcerted him partly because they went on having a good time together however energetically Finch adopted inertia. Finch was a man with no zone of indifference and a lifelong distaste for milky kindnesses, which made his present wish to push Henry away and into a career of his own both powerful and covert. What he would do without Henry, lord knows. His mild-mannered and gifted friend had a contagious sense of what was interesting, amusing, noble, or important in life, though his bearing was lugubrious, like a plumber's. Finch had always found him altogether reviving. Before they had met, both aged six, Finch seemed to have lived alone for eons. He was an only child who had learned to read at three and quickly began giving characters to the numbers in arithmetic because he had no one to play with. He devised adventures for them. The number one was reckless, two was intelligent, three was inclined to wickedness, four was heroic.

As time went on, Finch found himself more and more attached to bed. He read a lot.

His daily woman said in the butcher's that he wasn't poorly, he was taking a holiday.

"Some people!" snorted the butcher.

"Well, I daresay it's work really," said the daily. "He's doing a lot of thinking in his head. If looks are anything to go by, he's thinking in his head all the time."

Henry went to Ohio and gave the concert on his own. He telephoned Finch when he was back at his flat in London. Finch lived in Cheyne Row. Henry was about to move out of a place in Tite Street.

"You sound as if you're still in bed," Henry said.

"Why shouldn't I be?" said Finch.

"I've got the name of an analyst. A very nice man who's been struck off the register because he married a patient. And then she tried to kill herself but now she's all right. Fairly."

"You've got a nose for the washed-up, I'll say that for you. How do you know he's nice?"

"I've just had a drink with him."

"Well, I'm not going to him. There's nothing the matter with me."

"You should be up."

"I like it here."

"You'll run out of money."

"Not for a while."

"I've fixed for you to go and see him on Thursday. Or he'd even come to you."

"If he's offered to come to me, he can't be much good."

"I told you, he's been struck off the register. He's hard up."

"You do find them," said Finch.

"Then Thursday."

"No. I don't want another intimate. How many can a man have at a time? There's you and Betty. George, Peter, Anna. And there used to be Gloria, and I still have to think about her even if she isn't here. You don't not spend time on someone just because they aren't about any longer. That's six. I don't want some extra bogus friend."

"Gloria wasn't doing you any good."

"No, but I still miss her rather."

"So do I. I liked the way she muttered so you could hardly hear when she was being funny. Girls don't usually do that."

"Girls apart from Betty aren't usually funny."

"No," Henry said. He stalked about and thought. The receiver with Finch on the other end growled. He came back to it. "I've decided I'm not going to give another concert on my own until you start working again," he said.

Finch was so overcome by the brilliance of this counter-stratagem that he yelled. Then he said, "In that case you can bloody well go and waste your own bloody time seeing your half-baked analyst for me. You can tell him anything he could possibly want to know about me."

"I'd have to make up your dreams."

"Feel free," said Finch. He sulked then for a moment. "Or you could ring me up, couldn't you? You could ask me what *I'd* dreamt."

"No decent analyst would agree to it."

"He sounds a rotten one, so there's no problem, is there?"

"He's not rotten."

"I quite like nursery rows sometimes." Finch leaned back on his pillows and tried one. "Yes, he is rotten."

"Isn't.

"Is."

"Isn't."

"Is."

"Who says?"

"Says me."

"Who are you?"

"Finch James Borthwick hyphen Grantley aged twenty-eight

years two months three weeks. Anyway," Finch said in his ordinary voice and coming out of the interesting counterpoint,
"if he's not rotten, he's certainly out of the usual run of ana-
lysts. Most unrotten doctors haven't been struck off the register. As a generality."

"You're barking."

"Yes, I know. It's exhausting me," Finch said, though
sounding splendid. He went on, absorbed in the endeavor of
thinking of a ploy, "I'm worn out with all this." He thought of
the ploy. "Your harebrained idea of going to the chap instead
of me—"

"It was your harebrained idea," Henry said with heat.

"You shouldn't be going to some analyst every day for someone else," Finch pushed on. "You should be playing the
piano."

But Henry was hellbent on getting Finch up, hellbent
enough to go to the analyst on his behalf. Day after day.

"What dream did you tell him?" Finch asked from bed after
the first morning, trying not to sound too alert.

"The one you told me to tell him, of course."

"What did he make of it?"

"He doesn't seem to say much. I believe they never do.
They mostly make you talk."

"It sounds an awful effort."

"He wanted to know what *my* motive was, and I said I
didn't have many, and he said that wouldn't wash usually, but
perhaps in this case."

Another day: "What dream did you tell him? You didn't
ring."

"I couldn't get through to you. I hadn't got the change to

ring you from the tube, and I'd had to rush out of the house to get there because I woke up late."

"So what did you tell him?"

"One I'd had. I thought it would do. It was about our childhood, so you were in it. It was about the time you dropped the raw egg into your great-aunt's letter box."

"Wasn't that a good day," Finch said, closing his eyes in commemoration and then opening them to look fierce at the effrontery of somebody's making up his dream. "But I don't *think* about being a child."

"The analyst said it was a very bad sign. The raw egg."

"I daresay, but it was a very good day." Finch ambled back to his point. "I don't *think* about being a child, so it's not a plausible dream. I hated being a child, apart from knowing you. I wouldn't dream of dreaming about it."

"They say we dream a lot of things we hate thinking about in the daytime."

"Well, I hate *dreaming* about them too, so I don't. Asses."

The visits progressed. Betty often came to see Finch while Henry was with the analyst. He liked her. Henry's cat wandered into the bedroom one morning; Betty and her six-year-old son had brought it with them. Finch thought, bestirred, that the cat was an advance guard for Henry and that Henry must be on his way back to see them, and he wanted to call out to the animal, but in his excitement he couldn't remember its name, so he lay back and assumed fatigue again. The child, who had been watching him gravely, said, "Why aren't you playing the cello any longer with my father? Are you going to die?"

"No, I'm just tired."

"I expect you've got a sore throat," the boy said. "Would

you like some condensed milk? It's better than whisky and honey and lemon."

"Your father and I used to eat a lot of condensed milk when we were children."

"He's told me."

"Do you want some?"

"It's a bit sweet for me. I suppose it's O.K. if you're old," said the boy.

"We were getting on for ten when we liked it," Finch said. He felt animated; and then he remembered his obligation to be bedridden; and then he wondered what Henry was saying to the analyst, and whether his friend's loyalty and humor were visible to the man, and what was to happen next to them all. He turned over onto his side.

"What is it?" Betty said.

"I was hating the analyst."

"When you haven't met him?"

"I was wondering what I landed Henry with."

"He wanted to do it."

"I was wondering if the analyst is taking it out of him."

The boy honorably brought him a tin of condensed milk and a tin opener from the kitchen. Finch opened the tin and looked at it. The child went out of the room again.

"I was thinking about the irrelevance to psychoanalysis of wit and accountability," said Finch.

The six-year-old came back, carting a telephone directory. "I remember a number that I think might interest you," he said encouragingly, starting at the beginning of the book and going down the columns to look for it.

After a while, wishing to support the undertaking, Finch sat up on the side of his bed and played something buoyant on his cello. "It's not much without your father doing the piano part," he said.

"What part?" said the boy.

Finch got up, for the first time in company for many moons, and went to the piano in his drawing room next door, shouting "I can't do it properly." The pedals under his bare feet were interestingly strange to use and slightly painful. "Have you found the number?" he bawled to the child in the middle of a difficult run, thinking at the same time that the business of Henry's going to the analyst for him was actually doing the opposite of freeing his friend.

"Probably nearly," the child shouted.

Finch finished the movement and then came back to the other room, thinking of how much time he had spent with Henry and Betty over the years. "There's a special word in Russian for someone who moves in on a household indefinitely and has the right to complain about the arrangements," he said, "and I'm it." He climbed back into bed, laying the cello on the right-hand pillow, which was more practical since the telephone was on the left-hand side, and read some music while the child went on going through the numbers in the telephone directory.

"Almost any number you liked would be nice," Finch said.

"No," the boy said, not lifting his head. "It was the same backwards as forwards, and it had a six in it. It was a special one."

Henry came into Finch's flat one day and refused the usual catechism about what he had said to the analyst.

"You talk as if your dreams were, I don't know, pieces of new music," Henry said. "Sometimes you think you've done all right but often you say they don't hold water or they won't stand up. A man's *allowed* to have second-rate dreams if he feels like it. The dream you were lamming into yesterday was a perfectly good dream, the doctor said. He said you mustn't victimize yourself."

"Victimize!" said Finch.

"He said a lot of tyrannical people are really masochists."

Finch groaned and tried to go to sleep.

"Now what?" said Henry. "The man's doing his best. He's very nice about you. He bought your last record."

"*Our* last record."

"He's going through a lot because of your not wanting to see him."

There was a long pause while Finch committed murder in his heart, and then sat up in bed with his cello and played arpeggios.

"That sounds like a nutmeg grater," Henry said.

"Yes. I haven't been practicing. I've been in *bed* all this time. I'd been trying to go to sleep. I know: instead of going to sleep, let's go to Tunisia."

"Why Tunisia?"

"There's a letter asking you to play at an out-of-doors arts festival in the desert somewhere. I'd come for my health."

Finch walked about Tunisia in fur-lined bootees to emphasize his frailty. The bootees were unzipped to the anklebone because of the heat. The festival was a theatre-and-music fiesta devised for the villagers and attended by the experimental cognoscenti of the world, many of them Jews. Henry played the piano out of a van on forays into the hinterland to introduce the Trans-National Drama Research Gymnasium. Surprised villagers, grateful at first for free entry to anything, crept away from improvised stage sketches in a prepared nonlanguage. The directors and actors had spent months in zoos recording the noises made by apes in emotional situations. A man working on a theatrical seminar called "Computers—Whither?" was angry because the ape recordings had thieved some of his points about the place of computer speech in the new drama. At the same time, a filmmaker was directing an underground picture that owed a certain amount to *The Four Feathers* and *Lawrence of Arabia*. He was an agreeable man with a small private fortune and a look of poverty. Finch rather liked him. His name was Cecil Colling. Cecil had imported a tribe of Bedouins to the site to play the spectacular scenes. The men in the technical crew, unpaid, were earning their way by filming the fiesta for the B.B.C. The Bedouins, whom Cecil cared for and saw to be poor, were being paid in private out of Cecil's own pocket.

"The raid scenes are terrific," he would say after a day's shooting, flushed with love of his work. "The Bedouins are really getting the hang of it. So are the camels. When I fire one gunshot, they go. Two shots, they stop in a flash. You'd never find English animals as good as this. It's the speaking parts I'm having trouble with. Film's a visual medium; you can't get away from it."

Sometimes, when Henry was trying to write a letter of apology to the analyst for having quit, and wondering whether the man was all right—and when Finch was pondering the need to do the same thing—they would wander off together and watch Cecil coaching the people he referred to as "the speaking parts." It was against his convictions to call them "actors." The Bedouins and the camels, both groups equally bored, would gather round a portable gramophone of Henry's and nod to records of *On the Town* and Schönberg's *Moses and Aaron*, listening carefully while the sand blew into their faces.

An English statesman arrived for a feast he had arranged between the Jews present as guests and the Arabs who were their hosts. The meal was a gesture to compromise, lying in an

Anglo-Indian recipe for curry and a strawberry blancmange. The statesman knew he was going wrong somewhere: a kindly man, stocky, given to blunders, with misleadingly piercing blue eyes and a stoop. "Is that so?" he would say when he hadn't actually grasped a point; or sometimes "Quite." But people felt generally the better for his "Quite" at conferences, and so did the guests at his baffling feast. His presence was not a bad one to bestow, and his words carried across dead air with a kind of comfort. He would say "Is that so?" at the compromise meal, and immeasurable non-English-speakers would feel in touch with him. Or "Quite," and they would know what he meant. He had brought along with him an underling ex-ambassador, now in the U.N. Department of the Foreign Office, who was possessed of a sense of the fatuous that had often threatened to wreck his career. The statesman made a speech at the dinner. Finch was sitting next to the underling. The speech was in support of Arab-Israeli understanding. "Let the lion (whichever is the lion—I don't know)," said the statesman in a tactful bellow, "lie down with the lamb (whichever is the lamb—I don't know)." The underling sealed the end of his job by laughing. Finch had picked up some Arabic and heard the interpreter translating the image into a metaphysical one about a camel (whichever is a camel) lying down with a camel (whichever is a camel).

Loafing about Tunisia in his unzipped bootees, Finch missed his cello, among other things. The courtly interpreter of the festival, a Tunisian, after giving him some hashish jam, said to him in a tent that he hoped he had peace of mind.

"Yes. I have a prior attachment," Finch said, to his surprise, but thinking not to be understood.

"Attachment to what, if I may ask?"

"To railway carriages. To bikes. To Sickert." At home in Northumberland long ago, there had been a painting by Sickert whose poignancy and brilliance had stopped him nightly on his way to bed. Finch lay back, lulled by hash, and thought of the Botticelli in the billiard room and the Angelica Kauffman on the half-landing and the Landseer in the downstairs lavatory. Not a man to fall prey to fabricated regrets, he remembered clearly that the Angelica Kauffman was a bad one, and pondered the question of people's nerve to achieve the first-rate. Henry would never lack it.

In Tunisia, doing nothing, Finch mooched and grumbled and read, and what he was thinking about had room to expand. He found himself responding to some of the ideas that the Tunisians gently explored in their tents. Their attitude to life was not unlike Henry's, he thought. Finch had a temperamental dislike of the physical idols of Greek literature and of English public schools. He found only Ulysses deeply human, with his craftiness and patience, and Oedipus, who wished to find out the unaccommodable truth about himself, and Perseus, who kept his heart from turning to stone.

One night he wept with rage in the desert cold. That's what comes of not practicing, he said to himself furiously.

"What is it?" said Betty, who was with him, and Henry.

"I don't like the times. Bad times," he said, without meaning to.

"Have you been having hash?"

"No."

"What's wrong with the times, apart from politics?"

"We've got no remorse. Only guilt, that's the trouble. It's better here. It's also better in bed. And I like it with you two. What can one do in a time when no one is ashamed of having done something, when people are only guilty, as a weapon?"

"If you despised the times as much as you pretend, you

wouldn't be angry with them," Henry said. "You've got yourself out of bed. Now take off your bedroom slippers."

"They're boots."

"All right, they're in the historic line of Aunt Belle's cardigans in Tibet, but zip them up."

"Henry's found a cello for you," Betty said.

"I've given up the cello for the moment," said Finch.

"I can't imagine going on performing without you," Henry said after a wait. "I don't want to."

"Your nurse once said to you, 'Some can, some can't, some do, some don't, and you're a can and do.'"

"I don't remember that."

"It struck me."

Unwilling to act in his proper person, Finch went back to London and started to live too high. Henry rose to fame on his own. Bank managers and accountants tried to depress Finch, but for all the limbo he was in, his spirits were kept up by the strongest curiosity to see what would happen next. I am a pirate and an exhibitionist, he thought, but not a cynic. He remained the best of all friends to people. After Henry had outstripped him in celebrity, he grew riotous. Refusing to teach or to perform, he started to compose, which much pleased his daily, though no one else knew of it. By night he kept himself from the usual evenings with Henry and Betty, thinking to leave them some space for a time, and he would often take a sleeping pill at eight, before dinner, because sleep had grown difficult. On account of all the months in bed, no doubt, he decided. On top of even a glass of wine the effect of the sleeping pills was dramatic.

One evening, lonely, he was taken to meet a great harpsichordist of nearly ninety. She was known for her acerbity, her

cucumber sandwiches, and her insistence on decorum. It was
uncertain whether she was offering him tea or dinner or nothing, since the time she gave was a quarter to six and she
would never have had anyone to drinks. Out of nerves and
hero worship, he had three double Scotches before setting out
and two more on the way, and then made himself self-
destructively late by going into a greengrocer's to buy some
mint to chew so as to disperse the Scotch. He arrived, having
picked up his companion guests, in a vast flat in West Kensington. There were no carpets on the polished boards. Upright
chairs were placed around the walls of the drawing room a
large distance from one another. The great woman came in:
standing four foot eight, using a gold-topped cane. She sat
firmly on one of the upright chairs and spoke about the
breeding predicament of her mare. No one knew that she had
a mare.

"I was thinking of putting her to a very nice stallion I've
seen in the district," she said. "She's getting on, and it would
be pleasant to have a foal. She's nineteen. It isn't unknown to
have a foal at nineteen."

"Really?" someone said.

"I'm afraid I lied about her age to the stud farm. Do you
think it matters? I said she was sixteen." The old woman took
a lace handkerchief out of the tapestry reticule hanging from
her left wrist and rolled the handkerchief into a ball between
her hands, which was a gesture everyone in the room knew
from her concerts. "I daresay I shouldn't have done."

Finch lost his head and said to this woman whose fastid-
iousness he most revered, "You wouldn't lie about your own
age, that's the thing."

She gave him a basilisk gaze and he tried to dispose of his
long legs around the legs of the Sheraton chair.

Later on—days, he thought glumly—they moved into the

dining room, which was an equally august and unmerciful place. The sherry in the clear soup put him out entirely. When he woke up his hair was in the soup and his head on the rim of the plate, and his hostess had left the table.

"We'd better go," someone said. "We'll take you home."

"I don't want to go home," he said, quite out. His rescuers, a couple, decided to take him to Henry's new flat in Shepherd's Market, which Finch had prevented himself from invading.

"Num quid vis?" he said to them in the taxi. " 'Is there anything else you want?' It's what the Romans said when they assumed the answer was no. The answer is yes. A common leave-taking, they used to say at school. *Num* expects the answer no. *Nonne quid vis.* The Romans never said that, I think. People don't. *Nonne* expects the answer yes."

"We're dropping you at Shepherd's Market," the woman said loudly, as if to someone disabled. There's nothing wrong with me, Finch thought.

Henry and Betty took him in. He accepted them without noticing them or where he was, because of the naturalness of it and the sherry on top of shock. He spoke to them and they to him of books and girls and other things. His bulk, thin but long, was hard for them to get up their spiral stairs, so they left him on the sofa below, on the floor that lay over an ironmonger's shop. At six o'clock the next morning he came stumbling up their stairs, threatening to crack the banisters, having the strength and the weight of a buffalo. They heard him in the bathroom, running the water, then breaking a tumbler between long pauses.

After a great while his footsteps lumbered in their direction. There was a knock on the door.

"Come in," Betty said.

"Who is it?" said Finch, without opening the door and still knocking. "Whoever it is, I've been looking in your books and you haven't got your *name* in your books. Every other time I've been in somebody's flat like this I've known where I am by the books."

"Come in," Betty said again.

He opened the door. "Good lord," he said, hitting his head against the top of the door frame. "Oh my friends, I am glad it's you. It might have been anyone."

Property

➤➤➤ ➤➤➤ ➤➤➤ CHARACTERS: Max, Peg, Abberley.

SCENE: *An arc of pale sand-colored hessian reaches from floor to beyond eyeview. Three single beds, pinned to floor, equidistant. Peg's bed in the middle of the fan-shaped positioning. Iron bedsteads, beautiful; beige-and-dark-brown blankets; white linen. Small antique tables in polished dark woods beside each bed, stacked with belongings. Abberley's with piles of cigarettes, note pads, lawyer's folders, photographs, a torch, pencils, jar of caramels. Max's with a pipe, tobacco, scientific journals. Peg's with a few books, playing cards, solitaire board, jar of caramels. All have bottles of pills, booze, glasses, thermoses, radios, and earphones. At the foot of each bed what appears to be a miniature TV set faces the person lying on the bed. The machines are electrocardiographs. The wires recording from forearms and calves are not particularly visible for the time being. The three people not in nightclothes. Dressed to be ready at any time for expeditions and undertakings that will not actually occur. Peg in a gray-and-white print and some soft turban or scarf that hides her hair. Abberley in white shirt, city tie, black trousers. Max in gray flannel trousers and gray brawny pullover. All with bare feet. Shoes and socks by beds, neat. No other furniture. All are youngish and healthy. A separate spotlight is trained on each bed. When a character goes to sleep or withdraws from contact, his spotlight snaps off. There is also a perpetual faint natural light in this space where the three of them live immovably together.*

Four forty-five in the morning. The three are singing the last bars of a song. Exuberant mood. Sound rather soft. Pom-pom-pom. Peg carries the tune. "When you are in love, it's the loveliest night of the year. . . ." The waltz that grinds out of carrousels. The men do a unison dum-di-di bass. Slight shambles. Also triumph.

PEG: Now I want to do the—dum-di-di—bass. Abberley, do the tune.

MAX: It won't be any good that way. The two people doing the bass have got to be the same pitch.

PEG: Well, let's try. Abberley. (*Gives him a note.*) Max. (*Their note.*)

(*Abberley sings with his head down. Concentrated. Peg has her neck craned, like a dog baying at the moon. Max efficient and stolid. Born pipe smoker. Peg is married to Abberley.*)

ABBERLEY (*fast*): Now me with her. It worked fine. We were beautiful.

MAX: You mean I can have a go at the tune?

(*They sing. Subdued rowdiness. Hot drinks out of thermoses.*)

MAX: What time is it?

ABBERLEY: Getting on for five in the morning.

PEG: Oh good, it's Friday. Is it Friday?

ABBERLEY: No, my duck, we've barely embarked on Thursday yet.

(*Peg lies on elbow with her back to him, watching Max.*)

MAX: I think I'll relax for a while. We had a short night.

(*Max puts on radio earphones and leans back with eyes*

closed. The light trained on his bed snaps off. He remains faintly visible.)

PEG: Don't go to sleep. Notnotnot. We were having fun.

(*Abberley looks at her back.*)

PEG: He's left us. He's quit. God damn him. Are we done with?

ABBERLEY: No. I won't have it. (*Pause.*) Are we?

PEG: Shall we both take a small pill and sleep it out until later?

(*Silence. She takes a pill anyway.*)

PEG (*without looking at Abberley*): What could I do to cheer you up?

ABBERLEY: You're going to leave me, aren't you?

(*Silence.*)

ABBERLEY: I know you want to now.

(*Silence.*)

ABBERLEY: Why?

PEG: It's not as good as it was. I remember when it was wonderful.

(*Silence.*)

PEG: No, wrong. . . . I put that wrong. I don't mean that anything about us, about yourself and me, has fallen off. I mean longer ago than that. Much longer.

ABBERLEY: My dear love, you make yourself sound so old. I can't bear to hear you speak of yourself like that. You're very young.

PEG: I meant very long ago.

ABBERLEY: When you were with your *mother*? Good Christ. We must be better off together than that.

PEG: Don't be Freudian.

ABBERLEY: You're beautiful. Brush your hair.

PEG: Why?

ABBERLEY: I like watching it. Hell, why can't you do as

you're told for me? You know that's what you're supposed to do. (*Continues to sit up and watch her, rapt. But voice angry.*) Let me go to sleep.

(*Pause.*)

ABBERLEY: You're still lying there keeping me awake. Are you going to drop off or not? There are some manners left, not to speak of anxiety. I've got to see you out, haven't I? (*Pause.*) Apart from that, who'd pass up the chance of an idle moment together? Without him? (*Pause.*) All the same, if you're just going to lie there keeping me awake, I've got to go to sleep. It may not impress you, but there's a man I should be defending in court all day, and it's nearly dawn. (*Lies back.*) It's going to be dawn. You don't know what it's like, trying to go to sleep. (*Pause.*) Are you awake?

PEG: No.

ABBERLEY: Leave now, my darling, if you're going to, I beg of you. (*Pause.*) What's been the matter? I don't understand.

PEG: We've got too many things.

ABBERLEY: What the hell does that mean?

PEG: I'm probably wrong. (*Pause. Soft voice*) Somehow we landed up with too many things.

ABBERLEY (*shouts*): I've got to go to sleep! (*Pause.*) How do you expect me to go to sleep after you've told me something like that? What am I to do? Something terrible's going to happen.

PEG: Thursdays are never easy. In fact they're bloody awful. Shall we have some sardines? A headline yesterday said, "SATURDAY CANCELLED FOR LACK OF SUPPORT." (*Pause.*) I suppose it was a sporting event. A social event? Badminton? (*Fast*) Gliding? Jam-bottling? (*Pause.*) What a shame. *Saturday* unsupported. That's the best of them.

ABBERLEY: Shut up. I can't hear what you're thinking. (*Pause.*) I can hear you thinking something awful.

PEG: What could I do to stop you troubling?

ABBERLEY: Promise me not to— I could kill you for making me ask you that. One has no right.

PEG: Shall I come into your bed?

ABBERLEY: No room.

PEG: Are you O.K.?

ABBERLEY: That's my business.

(*He is gazing at his machine. So is she.*)

ABBERLEY: Get the sardines. Sardines would be nice. (*Pause.*) They wouldn't be forlorn, would they?

PEG: Eating in the night is never forlorn.

ABBERLEY: True. Then let's have caramels and you won't have to go away.

(*Peg starts to kick her sheet off.*)

ABBERLEY: Don't!

PEG: You can't stop me.

(*Abberley sighs, lies back, pulls the sheet up to his chin and pretends to sleep. Peg opens a drawer and gets out a nail file from a manicure set. The noise alerts Max. He watches. Anxious. She gets up and works on the screws pinning the legs of the bed to the floor. Her wires show. On all fours, she turns her electrocardiograph around in Max's direction, and ours. Max watches intently. Green track of pulsebeat bounces like a ping-pong ball. Abberley talks over her as soon as she leaves bed.*)

ABBERLEY: You can't do that, you'll come unplugged, we can't do it, in our condition, not fair, we can't be expected. Now I can't see your set. Damn you, what if you've stopped, how'm I supposed.

(*Abberley gets out of bed himself. Stands with his back to her, hands in pockets, looking at wall.*)

PEG (*still on all fours*): Stop pretending there's a window.

ABBERLEY: I'm thinking.

PEG: No, you're not, you're feeling, I can tell.

(*Peg tries to go over to Abberley. Wires won't reach. Stands at nearest point to him. Arms slightly forward.*)

PEG: I thought if I could push them together.

ABBERLEY: You're supposed to be someone I look after.

(*Silence.*)

ABBERLEY: Blast your energy. O.K., I know it's a miracle, yes, I'd be grateful for it if I were dead. I know it's the best thing that ever happened to me.

PEG: Well?

ABBERLEY: But I can't deal with it. Dear God. (*Pause.*) Rest His soul. (*Turns round, sees her machine now facing her bed again and in his view. Watches. Relief, then boredom. Max looks at it fixedly. Abberley leans against his bedhead. Tries radio earphones.*) They're talking about *food* on the *music* program. "Non-caloric . . ." My God. "Flaming kebab tonight on our own Excalibur." (*Takes off earphones.*) Putting out announcements like that before *breakfast*. What's going on out there? (*Gets back into bed.*) "Excalibur." Showoff. I can't stand pushy food. I like your food.

(*Pause. Abberley watches her. She is again on hands and knees.*)

ABBERLEY (*urgent*): I'm hungry. (*Pause.*) Girls shouldn't do things like that.

PEG: Well, you help, then.

ABBERLEY: I'll get a carpenter tomorrow.

PEG: Tomorrow!

ABBERLEY: What's tomorrow done?

PEG: What guarantee?

ABBERLEY: Darling, tomorrow comes over the hill in hordes, like the Chinese.

PEG: *You* believe that? Old blackheart? (*Sits back on heels.*) What a good day.

ABBERLEY: I was only trying out the idea. (*Pause.*) I seem to believe it as long as you're still ticking over nicely.

(*Peg goes back to work. Both men gaze at her machine.*)

ABBERLEY: Why won't you ever do what I say? That bed is pinned to the floor for a purpose.

PEG: Don't be religious.

(*Pause. Abberley looks for something by his bed.*)

PEG: What are you doing now?

ABBERLEY: My pen's gone.

(*Abberley shines his torch at her bedside table.*)

ABBERLEY: You've got my ballpoint pen.

PEG: I didn't know it was yours. No ballpoint can be *your* ballpoint. Ballpoints are *people's*. (*She sits on the edge of her bed.*)

ABBERLEY: Now what is it?

PEG: Darling, go to sleep.

ABBERLEY: How can I when you're wanting to move the bed and I don't want you to? (*A rush*) I've given you all this. We've got all this. It isn't enough for you, and I hate you for it, and I want you to go before you decide to leave me, and I love you, and how am I expected to stand being cooped up with him.

PEG: Yes.

ABBERLEY: Yes what?

PEG: That's what it's like.

ABBERLEY: Shut up. You're too young to decide that. You're mine. (*Shouts*) Where am I to live?

PEG: We've no choice.

ABBERLEY: You're where I live.

PEG: I'm here.

ABBERLEY: You're mine.

PEG: Things have changed.

(*Silence.*)

ABBERLEY: You've no business. You're too young.

PEG: I feel as old as the hills.

ABBERLEY (*weeps*): I decide.

(*Silence.*)

ABBERLEY: Could we have your lamp off? It's too bright. You will insist on these hundred-and-fifty-watt bulbs. It's like living in a bleeding watch factory. (*Looks at Max.*) Of course, there are times when he's company. As technologists go.

PEG: Do you think your eyes need seeing to?

ABBERLEY: You can't do this.

PEG: I'm in love with him.

(*Abberley whips head away. Pause.*)

ABBERLEY: I'll kill you.

PEG: I could go to a hotel for a bit.

ABBERLEY: Perhaps you won't have to go far.

(*Lights snap off.*)

--->>>

(*Lights snap on. Nothing displaced. Much time has passed. The three people look the same. Abberley talking cheerfully to Max. Peg dozing, her light off.*)

ABBERLEY: A lot to be said for it. No more upset nights. A man needs time to hide himself. Where is she?

PEG: I'm here.

ABBERLEY (*to Max*): How is she?

MAX: Fine.

ABBERLEY: I wanted to remind her about her driving license. It's expired and she never remembers.

MAX: You can always find us, God knows.

ABBERLEY (*chatty*): She came back for her books. She took a painting someone gave us as a wedding present. I'll have to get the wall repainted. The place is a wreck. (*Gestures at serene emptiness. No change, ever.*)

MAX: But she told me she didn't take a thing?

ABBERLEY: The paint's a completely different color underneath. Nasty patch. I'll never find anything the same shape. I'm supposed to be a lawyer. I haven't the time to go traipsing around art galleries. Where is she?

MAX: She should be at the dentist's all day tomorrow.

ABBERLEY: Her teeth are perfect.

MAX: She has four impacted wisdom teeth.

ABBERLEY: But no decay?

MAX: I'll ask her, if you like. It's not the usual thing we spend time discussing.

ABBERLEY (*addressing himself to his electrocardiograph*): Scientists are pompous asses. (*Turns to Max and shouts.*) As if you hadn't both got all the time in the world! (*Polite*) Could we all meet and talk someday?

MAX: What the hell else do we do?

ABBERLEY: I meant meet formally. It might make the difference? (*Pause.*) I want to give her a Christmas present. I thought it would go with her hair. As long as you don't mind. A cowhide rug. For you both, really.

MAX: Then what color is cow?

ABBERLEY: Have you forgotten? *All* cows are *brown*.

MAX: *Some* are black and white. Brown—scarcely—can scarcely be said to match fair hair.

ABBERLEY: *Fair*? Her hair was always brown. Quite a dark brown.

MAX: It's touched up. Tinted. What we used to call "dyed." Longer ago, what we used to call "helped."

ABBERLEY: She never dyed her hair when she was living with me.

MAX: It's gone gray. You haven't noticed. Peroxiding it seemed a hopeful idea. She did it after she'd been ill.

ABBERLEY: Nothing—is—ever—wrong—with—her. She's as

strong as a horse. Nothing was ever wrong with her in our day. She was going to outlive everyone.

(*Pause.*)

MAX: Fine woman.

ABBERLEY: Girl.

(*Max humors him and reads a book.*)

ABBERLEY: I suppose I should get somewhere to live. I really do need a place. This—this well-bred—nothing.

MAX: It isn't bad, though.

ABBERLEY: No. (*Pause.*) Nice of you.

MAX: Excuse me for asking, but what did you chat about when you were alone? I don't find chatting very easy. (*Pause.*) You've noticed.

ABBERLEY: You're necessary. It seems. (*Gracious*) No reflection on you. (*He gets out his torch.*) Do you mind?

MAX: Please.

(*Abberley goes over toward Peg's bed, trailing his wires. Studies her face in torchlight. Returns to his own bed.*)

MAX: O.K.?

ABBERLEY: Exactly the same.

(*Pause.*)

MAX: Do we really have to go through this nightly ritual?

ABBERLEY: It's not the easiest hour.

MAX: Do you find science fiction helpful?

ABBERLEY: Sodium Amytal.

MAX: Could I have some?

(*Abberley throws the bottle. They take a pill each.*)

MAX: Cheers. Down the hatch.

ABBERLEY: Life has its rewards.

MAX: What did you talk about? In the old days?

ABBERLEY: Hard to say. (*Pause.*) We just *talked*. Sometimes we spoke our minds, sometimes not. What are you asking? You could have heard it all, if you'd had the ears. We had quite a lot of laughs. She played the mouth organ. She liked that. I gave her a ridiculously expensive mouth organ one Christmas, much like a cocktail cabinet. Et cetera, et cetera. I know her very well. We never ran out of things to say. Is that what you mean? (*Chuckles.*) Are you in a blue funk about running out of things to say?

MAX: What *sort* of things did you talk about?

ABBERLEY: Well. (*Pause.*) Heavens, man. (*Pause.*) There was food, for instance. (*Pause.*) And her childhood, for another thing. She had a foul father. We had many a cheerful chat about that. He used to swing her by the leg to fortify her character.

MAX (*shaking his head*): Those methods never work.

ABBERLEY: And I suppose you could say it was.

MAX: Was what?

ABBERLEY: Fortified.

MAX: *What?* She's as weak as a kitten. I've never heard her argue back in her life. Can't you hear her teeth chattering in the night?

ABBERLEY (*not listening, smoking*): Yes, she's a salty fighter. *There's* one who knows how to whip up trouble and find out where you stand. That's the thing. Spine. You can rely on her for that.

MAX: Stop using the present tense.

ABBERLEY: Look, we still live together, don't we? We're still stuck in this place. (*Cordial*) Couldn't you murder it? If you weren't here, Peg and I could have beaten it.

MAX: My dear Abberley.

ABBERLEY: Don't you my-dear-Abberley me. You're a technological grease-swabber.

MAX: You don't know a thing about her any longer. I don't believe you ever did. She's a mouse. She's also getting long in the tooth and she's subject to migraine.

(*Abberley puts his hand to his head for a second.*)

ABBERLEY: I'm the better judge. We were married for the formative period.

MAX: She always told me you didn't believe in Freud.

ABBERLEY: No, it was *her* that didn't. (*Pause.*) Is that right? It's all screwed up.

MAX: She forgets, too.

ABBERLEY: Oh, no. Her memory is impeccable. Except for dates.

MAX: Not now. (*Kind*) She's changed, you see. It only proves my point.

(*Lights snap off.*)

➜≫

(*Lights snap on. Peg still in semidark. Some other dawn.*)

ABBERLEY: Where is she now? Max? Where now?

MAX: She's supposed to go into hospital.

ABBERLEY: Save us, what for?

MAX: Just a checkup.

ABBERLEY: When I left her— No, say, say, to put it another way, why not be kind, second husband, after all, when she left me for you, when she quit, she left in perfect repair.

MAX: Well, she's fallen into rack and ruin now.

ABBERLEY: You can't have looked after her. (*Fast*) You'll be telling me she's got arthritis next.

MAX: Rheumatism, a bit.

ABBERLEY: Oh, no. No. (*Pause.*) It's not right.

MAX: I never understand what you liked about her. She always says she irritated you. She says she behaved like hell to you.

ABBERLEY: It isn't like that at all.

MAX: Wasn't.

ABBERLEY: All right. I probably didn't pay enough heed. At the time. That's crossed my mind.

(*Abberley gets out of bed, trailing wires, and looks at Peg's cardiograph. Sits on the floor, watching it. Tries to get near her, but the wires won't let him closer than the bedside table. He looks at her pills.*)

ABBERLEY: She's got plenty of phenobarbital. We won't run out. (*Pause. Rage as he tries again to reach her.*) Rheumatism!

MAX: It's to be expected.

ABBERLEY: The hell it is. You can't be looking after her. Everything about her has always worked.

MAX: You talk about her like a landlord.

(*Abberley turns his back and goes to his bed.*)

MAX: Temper about the roof falling in. Woodworm. Dry rot. Maintenance. Power failure. Fuses. Normal wear and tear. To be expected, to be expected.

ABBERLEY: *You've let it happen.* You've let her wear out.

(*Pause.*)

ABBERLEY: She's beautiful. You should look at her. Young.

MAX: I live with her. She's showing the normal signs of middle age. You don't grasp. People deteriorate.

ABBERLEY (*snorting*): Peg?

MAX: I call her Margaret.

ABBERLEY: Good God. (*Pause.*) Does she answer to it?

(*Max gets up and sits on the edge of his bed and smokes a pipe. Pause.*)

MAX: Do you think we should be making more of an effort, or is this as good as one can manage? Considering what's against us?

ABBERLEY: We might listen to the radio for a time. Both of us.

(*Silence for a short while. Abberley alone listens to his radio earphones. Max sits thinking. Abberley takes off earphones.*)

ABBERLEY: It's nice to be able to talk, isn't it?

(*Max walks over toward Peg and looks at her. It means un-*

plugging his wires from his body. Done casually. That sort of man. He kisses her. Abberley watches, solicitous. He nods. Gets anxious about Max.)

ABBERLEY: Would you mind turning your cardiograph around a little so that I can see it?

(*Max swivels set. Dead screen visible to us. Abberley watches. Max plugs himself in again. Normal graph. Abberley is relieved.*)

ABBERLEY: How's sex, if I may ask?

MAX: Fine.

ABBERLEY: Good. (*Pause.*) I— She must have said this to you.

MAX: She doesn't talk unpleasantly about you. Or give anything away. Is *that* what you thought? (*Pause.*) If so, I'll wake her up. I won't be party to your bitching yourself on the sly. You can do it with her as a witness.

ABBERLEY: Hush. (*Max holds still.*) I'm a difficult man. Naggy. I could never stand the worry of her taking her wires off. (*Pause.*) So you might say sex was a bit thin in this two-thirds of the room.

MAX: That's anxiety.

ABBERLEY: I'm furious with you about her teeth. What have you been doing to her? Any operations you haven't told me about?

(*Peg wakes up. Her light snaps on. Cheery mood.*)

PEG: Hello, my loves. Oh, Christ, it's Sunday. Shall we have an aspirin at once? We'll need a bit of perking up.

ABBERLEY (*serious, to Max, after scrutiny of Peg*): She's exactly the same.

PEG: No.

ABBERLEY (*hiding face*): You mean there's sign of toll.

MAX: Of what?

ABBERLEY: Toll. (*Pause.*) How dare she suffer? You're lying again. I remember her. There wasn't a cloud. She was the sunniest girl I ever knew. Even in the mornings, heaven help me, when burbling isn't exactly welcome. (*Pause.*) Primarily, she belonged to me. Therefore, ultimately. (*Pause.*) She *cannot* have changed.

PEG: I'm long in the tooth and short in the breath. How about a drink before dawn breaks? (*Serious*) Nice to be together, isn't it? (*To Abberley*) Darling, I have changed. You won't like my hair, for a start. I've got thin. I'm not what I was.

ABBERLEY: You're *exactly* the same. You *haven't* changed. *He's* let you go, if there's any question of it.

PEG: What month is it? October?

ABBERLEY (*to Max*): There, see what I mean? I know her backwards. See why I had to remind her about the driving license? Does she keep the insurance premiums up? On her jewelry? I didn't give her enough. Nothing much. But she wouldn't like it to be gone.

(*Peg is playing patience on her lap. Smiles at Abberley. We can see bits of jewelry heaped in her night-table drawer. She is wearing some beads now, hidden for the moment under her clothes.*)

MAX: It's November. It'll be her birthday before we can turn round. Feel free to give her anything you like. We don't go in for presents.

(*Peg smiles again at Abberley.*)

PEG (*looking from one to the other. Speaking brightly to close the gaps, as if at a party*): So it's getting near Christmas. Is Christmas worse because of the activity, do you think, or because of God? It *can't* be the activity, can it? (*Pause.*) What are the lucky creeps doing out there? (*Pause.*) The thing that makes me believe in God is that there's a special kind of weather on Sundays. Only on Sundays. Muggy. Gives you a headache. There must be a God.

MAX: That's mood, my love, not weather, and the mood's because the shops are closed. (*Sucks pipe.*)

PEG: That's a housewifish thing to say. (*Packs up the patience and goes toward Max's bed.*) Brrr. I expect I woke up at the wrong time. It'll be all right.

(*Max gets up and takes off her turban. Long blond hair falls out. She plaits it. Her beads show.*)

MAX: Who gave you those beads?

PEG: They're the ones I always wear.

(*Abberley has looked away from her hair. Sad. But pleased about the beads. She sits on her own bed and watches him.*)

PEG: Are you all right?

ABBERLEY: Fine.

PEG: How's Ronnie?

ABBERLEY: Fine.

PEG: How's George?

ABBERLEY: Fine.

PEG: How're Joe and Lil?

ABBERLEY: Fine.

PEG: Is Bob fine?

ABBERLEY: Fine.

PEG: Who else is fine?

ABBERLEY: Most of us. (*Pause.*) What have they done to your teeth and your bones? What are these migraines?

PEG: Thy wife, goat, or mansion.

ABBERLEY: What?

PEG: Nothing.

ABBERLEY: You sound tired.

MAX: She isn't tired.

ABBERLEY: Stop translating for her. *We lived together*. We had a *life*.

PEG: You don't know me anymore. You won't look. You do too much remembering.

ABBERLEY: I don't remember a thing about you. I don't remember the clothes you wore, or your beautiful hair, or the sardines, or the mouth organ. I recall nothing. I haven't owned you for ten years. Sixteen?

PEG (*to Max*): Stop him.

ABBERLEY: I gave up the title to you.

PEG: Max, help.

ABBERLEY: Dyeing your hair. Which side of the bed do you sleep on now?

MAX: *I* sleep on the right-hand side of my particular bed. When we share it. The right, seen from the head end.

ABBERLEY: So she's on the left. You've tried to change everything about her. She was on the track, don't you see? I don't believe she's better off. I have an idea of her. You're trying to take it away with all these dentists and bone men and switching her side in bed. Does she still drink tea all the time?

MAX: Yes.

ABBERLEY (*to Peg*): I told you you should take the Georgian teapot.

PEG (*tender*): I told you I couldn't be cumbered. (*Pause.*) How is it?

ABBERLEY: What?

PEG: Our teapot.

(*Peg and Max now begin to speak to each other. Abberley takes off his watch and looks at it. Notes time carefully. Puts watch on table and records the time on a pad.*)

MAX (*to Peg*): If we weren't having a civilized drink together, I'd bash you for that "our teapot."

(*Peg hums.*)

PEG: These are the middle years.

ABBERLEY: In a part of Greece, a remote part, a man who kills another man takes over the dead man's wife. Immediately. The care of her. The property. The sexual rights.

MAX (*to Peg*): Make him shut up. What about all humming again?

ABBERLEY: It's an intelligent union of heroics and economics. From the point of view of the man left alive.

PEG (*to Max*): Dear, you can see he is making an effort. Should we have a game?

(*Max attends to the interminable pipe. Silence.*)

ABBERLEY (*to Peg, accusing, grieved*): You've got other aches by now, I suppose.

PEG: I'm falling apart. The whole fabric. I need a relief fund. (*To Max*) Why don't you draw something?

ABBERLEY: I'd better leave you together. Not that one can move. (*To Peg*) You're no further off than you were, I suppose.

(*Pause.*)

PEG: The way I might have cared for you. . . . The people I could have done things for. . . . The place used to be lousy with them. Shall we have a drink? I don't feel very well.

ABBERLEY: You've let her rot away.

PEG (*to Abberley*): Are you frightened of dying at the moment?

ABBERLEY: Of you being ill. (*Looks at Max, covertly.*) Sh-h-h. Not now.

PEG (*to Max*): I'm sorry.

(*Max shakes head. Smiles.*)

ABBERLEY: We're not doing badly. We're having a drink. (*Pause.*) My dear, the time we had—it wasn't what we meant. Some. Not enough of it.

PEG: No. (*Pause.*)

(*Abberley looks at his own cardiograph for a time. Then turns it to us, away from himself, Max, Peg. Gets back into bed and looks at Max's machine instead.*)

PEG (*speaking to air in outrage*): I can't see it. He must know I worry if I can't see it. How dare he not know that?

MAX: Oh dear, now you're going to get upset.

ABBERLEY: Don't get upset. Would you like one of my pills?

PEG: I'm *not* upset. Yes, I would. (*To Abberley*) Are you all right?

ABBERLEY: Fine. (*Throws pills to her.*) Would you like my solitaire board? I've got too many things. My eyes hurt. I've got earache. I wish it would buck up and be Monday. Lousy dump. (*Pause.*) Perhaps I could yet do better. Scrap the thing so far and begin another. Something I could bring to a decent conclusion. One gripes and holds off and bangs the pillows and thinks the real thing is to come, and then one starts to lose the thread. My dear friends, this is it, yes? This. I realized that at a particularly good moment, at five forty-eight this morning. I took account of the time. Something pleasant happened. . . . Peg, I've grown immensely fat. You may notice it under the sheet. Clean sheets a great comfort, eh? (*Laughs.*)

PEG: Getting old has its funny side, I grant you that.

ABBERLEY: Would you do me the goodness of turning your electrocardiograph around to me? In honor of our—past. Away from him. Until it's light.

(*Crawling to bottom of bed, Peg turns the machine round to him.*)

ABBERLEY: Can we switch the spotlights off?

(*Spotlights snap off. Pale light through scrim wall. Max reads by a torch under the sheets. Peg crawls back to do the same.*)

ABBERLEY: You still have a very nice rump. The rump is often the first to fail.

(*We see the three electrocardiographs recording. Abberley's faces us. The two other machines face him, diagonally visible to us; Abberley watches them.*)

ABBERLEY: Thank you.

Foreigners

➤➤➤➤➤➤➤➤➤ "Oh god, I wish the shops were open," said the great atheist economist, near tears, to his terror. It was an ice-cold June Sunday. He had eaten roast mutton and apple charlotte. Three people in his Wiltshire drawing room slept, and so did his dogs. He looked at the fire hard enough to dry out his eyeballs, or perhaps to singe them.

"Sundays are impossible. I can't stand Sundays," his voice said, again frightening him. The voice was shouting. His hands were shaking. Sunday lunch, sleep; radio, muffins, sleep; gin-and-lime, the cold roast, radio, sleep. His English life, his English wife. On the opposite side of their English fireplace, Sara was answering letters on her engraved English note cards: "Mrs. Thomas Flitch, the Dower House." And so on and so on. His Indian mother was in a wheelchair by the bay window, reading. The sight of her brought back some Sunday in India. Himself a child on a bicycle. Dusk, nearly dark. Groups of young men sitting on the ground near a closed library, reading and talking by the light of flares in petrol cans.

His stepson, Simon, a tall stockbroker, guffawed for no obvious reason and kicked the chin of a sleeping dog off a pile of Thomas's books, although he didn't go on to pick up any of the spilled books.

"It'll be Monday all too soon," Sara said, with the brotherly grimness that Thomas had learned to read in her as a style of intimacy. Now she was doing household accounts and checking the milk bill. She looked fatigued and drawn. He loved her, and wished to save her the frightful inroads of Anglo-Saxon activity, and hated her hat. She was still wearing the ugly straw that she had put on for morning church. She had cooked the lunch in it. Thomas liked her hair and loathed all her hats. In fifty-odd years of high regard for Englishwomen and awe of the fortitude and grace he saw in them, he had never accepted their defiling hats.

Simon's daughter, Pippa, a beauty of six who had one blue and one green eye, swarmed watchfully into the room on her stomach with Thomas's encouragement and bounced up with a war whoop behind the chairs of two sleeping visitors. So she was as oppressed by Sunday as he was. He admired her for dealing with it so capably. There was an interlude of chaos. A pot of coffee was spilled, and Sara had to get a damp cloth for the trousers of one of the visitors, who was involved in an unwise pretense that he hadn't actually been asleep. Thomas seemed to be seeing things through the wrong end of a telescope. People appeared to be very small, and their voices were too loud for their size. Pippa was much scolded.

"I've brought something for Great-Granny," she said several times, while the storm went on around her pigtailed head and finally spent itself. She heard her father and Sara out, and meanwhile held the present in her closed hand.

After five minutes, Simon attended to what she was saying and assumed a look of astuteness. "Have you got something in your hand?" he asked. Pause. "Something for Great-Granny?" he carried on shrewdly. "Let's have a look at it, in case it's one of the things Great-Granny doesn't eat." He tried to force open her fingers. "Let Daddy tell you. You're old enough to know by now that in the country where Great-Granny comes from they don't eat some of the things we eat. It's not that they're fussy, it's because they think it's wrong. You know that now, don't you, Pippa?"

"You told me before," said Pippa.

"Ah, yes, you see; it's a chocolate. So we're all right. I thought so. Why didn't you show it to me in the first place? Run and give it to Great-Granny," he said, sometime after Pippa was already there. "Granny, Pippa's brought you a special chocolate," he went on, some time after the old lady had thanked the child.

Thomas's mother was named Arathra Chib. Although his father had acknowledged the son in due time—when the boy grew up to be phenomenally educable—he had never married Miss Chib. She had stayed in a Delhi shack made of biscuit tins and a tarpaulin. Mr. Flitch, not a bad man, had worked most of his life in India in the tea business. When his bastard turned out to be studious, the boy was accepted into the English bachelor's house for a short time before he was shipped off to prep school and public school in his father's country. He spent the holidays in England with any parents who would have him. If nothing worked out, he lived in the empty school. Some master, equally lonely, would be set to giving him extra essays and physical training to keep him occupied. Thomas bore England no grudge for the youth it dealt him; on the contrary. After getting a double first at Oxford he married Sara, scarcely able to believe his luck. She was a pretty young widow with a small son, and Thomas went to law to give the little boy his own surname.

"Well done, Pippa. Chocolates are perfectly safe," Simon said laboriously in the direction of the wheelchair.

Thomas was already in the grip of a disorder not at all na-
tive to him, and now he suddenly confounded everything he
believed he felt for Simon by remembering with hatred one of
his adopted son's practical jokes. Some like Sunday long ago,
the child Simon had crept up to his Indian step-grandmother
when she was asleep in the same wheelchair and thrown a
blanket over her, shouting that she was a canary in a cage.
Thomas had kept the memory at arm's length until now, when
it occurred to him that Simon's sensibility had not much
changed. The insight cracked Thomas's heart slightly before
he got rid of it again.

His mother's vegetarianism had been carefully respected at
lunch, with the usual faint suggestion that it was aberrant and
therefore embarrassing, although Sara did try to conceal her
opinion. Before the apple charlotte, Miss Chib was given a
bowl of pea soup with a spoonful of whipped cream on it.
Thomas had noticed the cream, which represented effort. It
also represented license, an unusual small expense on a treat
beyond the necessities of Sara's food budget. Though Thomas
was greatly revered he had never been well off, and now that
he had retired from government advisory jobs he earned nothing much except by writing. Simon, who was well on his way
to becoming a millionaire through his dealings on the stock exchange, had leaned over his pleasant young wife to peer at his
step-grandmother's plate. "I say," he said jovially, "I see my
mama's been lashing out a bit."

Thomas's house, which he could barely keep up, was run
mostly on the income from a small chain of modern toy shops
that he had built up for his wife over the years. He had given
her the capital for the first one on their twentieth wedding an-
niversary, when he had already bought a Georgian pendant
that he dearly wished her to have, but before he chanced giv-

ing it to her he had asked her what she would like, and she told him. She had ideas about how a toy shop should be run in these times. Strong plastics, instructive building toys, things that would save women trouble. After a long while of keeping the pendant hidden and unlooked at in his sock drawer, Thomas had to bring himself to hunt for someone to buy it back, for he couldn't afford both presents. He got nothing like the price of it. But Sara's idea had obviously been the better one, he told himself, though without believing a word of it, for where would they all be now without "Mama's business venture," as his stepson warmly pointed out to him on a walk round the garden this afternoon.

"Why don't you let me take over the accounts?" Simon said.

"What accounts?" Thomas asked, sheltering in slow-wittedness. He seemed to be fending something off. Nothing he was doing was like himself, and Simon looked at him oddly before poking a black pig in the belly.

"You should keep more pigs and run the place as a farm," Simon said. "And all this could be plowed up, too." He gestured across the lawn that ran down to a stream and then up again to his own cottage, which Thomas had given him as a wedding present. "The expenses of this place are ridiculous. Mama's a Trojan, but she's looking pretty whacked."

"She needs more help. I must see about more help."

"As I say, I could do the papers of the business. You wear yourself out with them."

"They seem to be taking longer at the moment. You wouldn't have time."

"Oh, I could do them on the train to the City some morning every week."

That fast? He probably could.

Simon looked around at the bigger house with an alert eye.

"This place is potentially a gold mine. It's madness to run it as a private house. If you turned it into a business, you could keep six maids and gardeners if you wanted and write them off against the pigs. Or whatever else you went in for. Mama's been talking of sugar beet."

Sugar beet? Sugar beet hadn't come up. Thomas steadied his eyes on the Tudor stable yard and his library window. "I won't have it," he said, shaking.

"Buck up, Father. Nobody thinks it's your fault. You're one of the world's thinkers. Been doing much writing?"

Thomas lied, against his temperament. "Quite a bit." Pause. "Preliminaries." Oh, come off it. But the ground seemed to be moving away. He felt as if Simon were lifting him by the collar and dangling him so that his feet were off the earth and his toes straining to reach something. Simon's big head and loose mouth loomed above him against the ridiculous English summer sky, which was the color of iron.

"Your last book was very impressive," Simon said. "Prunella and I both thought so. Reflected glow, you know." He blew his nose on a red spotted handkerchief that he wore in yeoman moods. "A bit above my level, I'm afraid, some of it."

"Oh dear. Was it hard to follow?" Thomas asked, taking him to mean what he said. "Which passages?" But Simon had never got beyond page 27, and after that he had merely left the book out in case his mother and stepfather came unexpectedly for drinks. So now he was at a disadvantage, which angered him, and he lost sight of the gratitude he usually summoned up for the stepfather who had spent much of his life obliging his adopted son's ambition for parents with a big house and a dashing car. At many moments of weakness, or love, Thomas had spent far more money than he could afford or even wished for the sake of Simon's joy in the holidays. The days when he could do it, or would, were now over. Their town house had been sold, lingeringly, with rearguard modernizing actions to keep up its price. The eventual loss kept Thomas awake at night. For the present, in the daytime, he was abruptly fed up with the lot: himself, his insufficiency, the toll that his financial state seemed to be taking of his wife, and the colossally polite head of his stepson, hanging over him now as if it had a miniature keg of brandy around its neck.

"Men are not made better by calamity," he said. At the same time, he was engaged in disliking his own state of intellect at the moment, which appeared to own no responsibility for the production of that sentence and buzzed around small problems without much resource or repose.

"What's that from? Is it an Indian saying?"

"What? No. Where was she thinking of putting the sugar beet?"

"Hey, I say, chin up. No calamity in this house, eh? Mama's full of beans."

"She's very tired."

"Take her to the sun. Take her to Greece. A friend of mine's got a yacht. You could charter it."

"It would be rather ludicrous." When we can't afford someone to clean the house, Thomas added silently.

"I could put it against the farm and it wouldn't cost anything. A conference yacht." Simon laughed loudly. "Mama could be entertaining foreign buyers. I do think you should let me go into the pigs."

Thomas told Simon to leave. He said he had work to do. Simon walked down to the stream and across the bridge to his own cottage, waving with his usual cordiality, which was unfailing because it depended on no cordial impulse. Thomas came back past the drawing room. He could see his mother, playing with Pippa, and his wife talking to a woman friend by the window. Thomas looked at them all, and then at Simon, who was now a small figure and in another sense no longer monstrous, because he was walking exactly as he had done when he was a very young child and most moving to Thomas, with his hands in his pockets and his back arched. The familiarity of everyone eased the strangeness in Thomas's head. I wish I had them all here, he thought. I wish we were together. I wish we were having a picnic, and that it was hot, and I do indeed wish that we were all together; though even if I were to hold the whole world against my chest, it would probably save us from very little. The longing was unaccustomed. He came to the drawing-room window, which was open. His mind had at last found its way back to its usual cast when he heard Sara's friend talking to her.

". . . start bestirring himself, for heaven's sake. Leaving you to do everything. What's a brilliant mind—"

"He is brilliant, that's so," Sara said over her. "But he's never made the career he could have done. He won't use his elbows."

But I am not that man, Thomas thought, shivering in a heap on the flower bed where he had dropped onto all fours so as not to be seen. I am not that man, he thought again, straightening up now, for in the next instant it seemed entirely necessary that he should not hide, should visibly walk to the front door and into his library. I will not be that man. He sat behind his desk for a long time, skipping Sunday's cold-mutton supper, rousing himself to say goodbye to the visitors, trying to deal with the paperwork of Sara's business. Wholesale and retail prices, markups, running expenses, employment insurance. Nausea. Sara, beautiful Sara, appeared in the accounts as the manageress. Deductible, to be candid. *No. Once not.* She had left samples of toys and plastic playthings among his books and manuscripts. Garbage. Her piercing household face swam across his eyeline, even more changed from its former self than now, and hermetic in its enthusiasm for nursery objects properly researched by child psychiatrists to be fit for the middle-class children who would lose them without a pang. There was a pale-pink celluloid rattle on his desk. It was decorated with an overdressed pale-blue rabbit in non-toxic paint. Long ago, he had found Simon a Hindu rattle made of chased silver with an ivory handle shaped for a child to hold. *What shall we leave behind us,* he thought. He stared at a Rajput scene on the wall among his books. "Won't use his elbows." I know as little of love as I do of painting, he thought. The days of smoking a pipe suddenly came back to him, and he realized that he was biting down on his own teeth. His mind seemed to be acting like mercury. He saw it slipping around in a pool and then dividing into drops that ran apart. He leaned back often for a rest and once he got up to type an envelope on an old typewriter in the window. The typewriter had been made in Delhi many years ago, copied from an English Underwood and reproduced in every detail except for the vital spring to drive the keys back. In the machine's heyday, the deficiency had not been regarded as crippling. Labor was cheap, time ran slow, and a girl sat beside the man typist to return each key by hand as he pressed it. Thomas had grown up in the neighborhood of the machine and one day he had bought it, bringing it to England by boat and vaguely intending to explore the possibility of supplying a spring, though he also liked it well as it still was.

He delayed going upstairs for as long as possible, partly in a hopeless pretense of getting the papers finished with, and partly to avoid Sara. But she was lying awake. He guessed her to be worrying about money. Temper defeated pity and he attacked her rabidly for, of all things, going to her Anglican

church. It appeared to him suddenly that there was a link between her flouted ambition for him and the ethic of a religion
more alien to his own thought than he had ever dreamed. He
sounded to himself like some tendentious student with balloon
words coming out of his mouth.

"Jesus was the first Catholic and therefore the first Mr. Success of the profit motive," he said, putting on his dressing
gown and feeling foolish. "Christianity and capitalism are in-
separable. Why do you go? Why do you spoil Sundays?"

Sara said, "You're not well. You're losing your grip." She
watched him quite carefully. She got up.

"I daresay. We can't stay in this house. We simply can't
keep it up."

She was quiet.

So he snarled. "Does it mean that much to you?"

"What do you think?" Now the rage poured out: All these
years, our things, deserve, owe, our time of life, all we've been
through.

Help, he thought. I can't go on. I can't manage any of it.

Earn, she threw at him.

Relearn, he thought, adding the first three letters to her
word in his head as if they were playing a game. "Church!" he
shouted.

"You never shout," she said, staring at him.

"You spoil Sundays!"

"Socrates was the first man who thought about thinking,"
she said, sitting on the window seat and surprising him in
every way.

"Uh?" he said over her.

"Jesus may have been the first man who understood the
power of some actions. The power of forgiving an enemy, for
instance."

"You mean me, don't you?" He held his head.

On Monday, when Sara had left the house early to see to things in two of the toy shops on the other side of the county, he could find nothing at home that he felt up to doing. He drove to a café in the nearby market town and simply listened to pacify himself. It was a tea shop, with one half that sold honey and homemade scones and the other with tables where the walls were decorated with a mixture of horse brasses and psychedelic posters. One of the middle-aged women who kept the shop had ordered a set of posters about the Paris rising of May 1968, because she had gone to the Sorbonne to study when she was a girl. The tea shop was next door to one of Sara's branches. Remorse had drawn Thomas there and it kept him pinned, though he was also wild for flight. An arthritic woman came into the café, alone, with a paper bag carrying the name of Sara's shop.

"You feel safer at home than what you do further away," she said after a long silence, addressing no one. "Further away you might be a nuisance."

Unplaced impatience felt like burrs on Thomas's skin. He leaned over to her and said, "No, you should get out and about more," which affronted her. He had broken the fourth wall.

In the late afternoon, slow to go home, he dropped in on an elderly doctor friend and played tennis. His hands shook and his friend prescribed a sedative.

"Work a strain at the minute?" said the doctor, watching.

"That sort of thing."

"Take two a day," said the doctor. "Sleeping all right?" The whole circumstance startled him. He expected limitless serenity of a man half Indian, and indeed Thomas had sustained the expectation for twenty years or more.

"Mostly," Thomas said.

"Let me know. Keep in touch."

"I can't concentrate. I don't understand myself. Sara's being a brick."

"Your English is more English than mine," the doctor said, not really to make conversation but to find more time to see. Thomas's mind seemed to be elsewhere, and there was no perfunctory laugh in return.

The doctor was concerned enough about him to trail him on a journey that Thomas then made to London Airport. He merely sat at the coffee counter there, hour after hour, alone. The talk of strangers alleviated something. At one point, he inquired at the Air-India desk and made a booking. Then he went back to the coffee counter, where two girls were talking about pop singers.

"I wouldn't mind marrying Paul," said the blond girl of the pair. She had a beautifully high forehead and an upper lip that twitched softly, like a cow's in a fly-ridden summer.

"Paul?" said her freckled friend. "Ringo any day."

"I think Paul's sweet."

"Ringo's more of a husband. More masterful."

"Well, if you're talking about *masterful*," the blonde said vaguely.

"Don't you want to be mastered?"

"Not much."

"I don't think a marriage with Ringo would work if he wasn't the master."

"There's always divorce."

They paused, and then the freckled girl said, "What about the cooking? I can't see me cooking."

"I wouldn't mind doing Paul a steak," said the blonde. "Or spaghetti. As long as it wasn't fish with the eyes left in, or a chicken. Not a whole chicken. Nothing with innards."

"Would you look after him if he was ill? That's what I'd

have to do for Ringo, you know. I wouldn't mind. I should think he'd be very demanding. Anyone in the public eye."

"Paul's kept his sincerity. He's not spoilt."

Thomas quietly bought them another cup of coffee each, and they giggled when they realized it and clinked the thick coffee mugs with him before carrying on with their conversation as if he weren't there.

"What sort of ill, anyway?" said the blonde.

"Sick, say," said freckles.

Thomas saw Sara in his mind's eye. She was never ill, but now she looked beaten and angered by something he must be doing to her. For richer, for poorer.

"What sort of sick? English sick or American sick?" said the blonde.

"What's the difference, then?"

"Cor, don't you know that? American sick is just ill. When they mean English sick, they say throw-up sick or sick to your stomach."

"English sick."

"Come to think of it, I'd look after him anyway. So long as he didn't carry on about it. You wouldn't catch Paul carrying on."

They ran for their plane, thanking Thomas for the coffee. He missed them and paced around and made another booking at the Air-India counter, stalling grandly about actually buying the ticket without even noticing that the people on duty were the ones who had humored him before. After a time, his doctor friend had seen enough of his extremity and took him for a drink in the airport bar.

"Funny, meeting you," Thomas said, refusing any ordinary guess that it could be no accident.

"Off somewhere?" said the doctor.

Thomas suddenly started to shake so badly that the ice in

his glass chattered. He fished the cubes out and put them into an ashtray and found it all he could do not to weep at the mess they made with the ash.

"You need help," his friend said.

"What for?" Thomas said. "The pills will do the trick. It's mostly that I can't sleep."

"There are things that pills don't do so well as a rest and treatment. You need a rest."

A county hospital treated Thomas that week for acute depression. He was greatly humiliated. He was also in fear. To the family, who were breezy, referring to "Daddy's trouble," he revealed nothing. Sara drove him scornfully to the hospital three times a week, for he wasn't supposed to drive. This on top of everything else, she seemed to be thinking, although she did what she might to eliminate exhaustion and scorn from her voice. On the car journey, which took an hour and a half each way, he would talk to her with all the will he could muster about the toy shops. It was barely manageable. He found it impossible to believe that he had ever been able to write a book, or give a lecture, or advise a government. Other scholars heard that he was unwell and sent him notes made remote by their instinct that his straits must mortify him. Sara felt many things, including affection, balked control, trouble over his loss of weight, and enmity toward one of the weak. Sometimes she tried talking to him about India, with a genuine impulse to do what she could. She did not feel shame, or any sense of partaking in the very view of life that was nearly extinguishing him.

At the end of the hospital treatment they went away to the Caribbean on holiday, by an airplane that belonged to a director of Simon's firm. An old friend of Thomas's lived on the island, but he was a Negro politician with a mind in the world that Thomas had lost for the moment. Sara had letters to people who owned polo ponies and valuable land for development. So Thomas played bridge with them, and swam, and learned to use an aqualung. He began to feel like a king, more or less. Or fit, at the least. One day he slipped off alone, out of interest, to look up a local doctor, who took him on a tour of hospitals. Maternity wards with two women to a bed. Children with rickets. He didn't tell Sara much of it.

When they got back to England Simon had a surprise waiting. He had exchanged houses with them. Sara and Thomas were to be in the cottage, and Simon's household of three in Thomas's place. The point was the running expenses. Most of the move had been accomplished already. Sara knew of it. "We didn't tell you, because you were too ill," she said. "We decided to wait, so that there was a secret for you when you came back. When you were your old self."

"It's a fine idea," Thomas said to her, expounding it to himself and meantime walking around Simon's cottage with resentment for every stone of the place. "They're an expanding family. There's less work for you to do here. It's very good of him. Where will I work?"

"I thought you'd be relieved. The financial burden. Young shoulders. Besides, he can write a lot of it off against tax, you know. So it's better in every way."

(*Where will I work?*)

"It's very good of him," he said, going across to the window to look at their house and then turning away in pain. He went on to bump his head on a beam. His state of mind was so much lighter than before that he laughed. "If *I* hit my head, at five foot nine, no wonder Simon wanted to switch," he said.

"It has nothing to do with his height," Sara said stiffly.

The only things left to be moved were Thomas's books. The Sunday after they came back from the West Indies, he and Sara and his mother—who was living with them now in a room not much larger than a cupboard, although the view, as Simon constantly said, was staggering—went formally to lunch in their old house. Sara started off in her hat, left on from church.

"For heaven's sake, take your hat off," Thomas said.

"Do you need one of your pills, dear?"

"No, I just hate your hat. We're going to our own house, aren't we? We're not going out."

"We are going out. You've got to adjust. The doctor said that about the income." This was the way she spoke of it: "The income." She meant his earnings, not the yield of the toy-shop business, but she had never been in the habit of referring to them so distinctly, let alone to the fact that they were thin on the ground at the moment. "We *are* going out. We're lunching with Simon and Prunella in their new home."

He threw a bottleful of his pills into the kitchen sink and tried to get them to go down the drain with the handle of a dishmop. "I hate the word 'home,'" he said. "It's like 'doggy.' The place is a house."

"It is my language," Sara said. She saw then that saying this had been unpardonable, but the odd thing was that he did pardon her, and laughed, and quietly fished some of the soggy pills out of the sink in case he fancied one later after all.

Simon was sitting in Thomas's armchair, which was too big to be moved to the cottage. Prunella had nicely been trying to prise him out of it before they came, but she was timid of him. "Better not to make an issue of it by my shifting," Simon said. "No need to treat him like an invalid."

At lunch, where there were maids to serve, Sara kept watching Thomas's plate. "Eat up," she said when he left something.

"No, thanks."

"The stomach shrinks. He's doing very well. He's put on six pounds," she told the table. She looked splendid herself, said the table. She did. But it seemed to Thomas that she was too doughty for him, somehow, and the hat finished it. For years and years, her frailer beauty had made him feel physically famished for her, but he had generally subdued the longing because she seemed worn out with housework. And now she was as strong as a cart horse, and he didn't give a damn. He suddenly felt farcically drawn to Simon's Prunella, which seemed a sign of health if nothing else.

"What's the joke?" Prunella said gently.

"There's a Russian story about a peasant who dreams night after night of having a bowl of cherry jam and no spoon to eat it with. And then at last he goes to bed with a spoon, and he doesn't dream."

Simon poured some port into the Stilton and talked of a hot tip about buying shares in a firm called North-East Gas Enterprises Limited. Thomas got up at last from his new place in the middle of the table, which he had quite liked because it had leg access to a rung where he could wriggle his feet when he was bored. He went to his old library, and Pippa followed him, equally enlivened to leave.

"Would you like to see my filthy sculptures?" she said.

"Very much," he said.

"They're in your library." They were made in Plasticine, and obviously based on photographs of Hindu sculpture in the art books on his bottom shelves. The six-year-old instinct had made them curiously abstract, and Thomas was much moved. The two were poring over them when Simon came into the room. He absorbed the little gray figures in a few seconds and his face bulged. He left the library and came back with a riding crop. Thomas found it hard to believe. He tried to block things but they went fast. The little girl was held by the back of her bent neck, and the lash of the crop swished down onto her cotton dress. When Thomas tried to grab the child away, the lash caught him in the eye.

"Stop!" he shouted, reaching again for the child and closing his red-hot eye.

"You speak of stopping," said Simon. "You led her on. Five, six, seven." It went on to nine before Thomas put an end to it. Simon by then had heavily said, "This hurts me more than it hurts you" to Pippa, and when the chaos was over Thomas began to laugh, for he had seen that the lash of the crop literally had curled round onto Simon's back between each stroke, probably quite stingingly, though the man had been too excited to notice it. Picking up the child, who was breathing in gulps like an oarsman at the end of a race, Thomas bent down to save her sculptures and carried her through to her mother. "I want these kept always," he said, thrusting the figures at her face.

"What are they?"

"They're sculptures of Pippa's. They're to be kept in my library. My books are to stay, too. I have a lot of work to do and there isn't enough room in the other place."

Sara said, "What was all that noise?" She looked more closely at the figures and turned away from him.

"What is it?" he said, watching her and flooded by a feeling that he had not expected. "You're not weeping?"

"You don't seem to be any better than before." She bent a little to lean her fists on the window seat, with her back to him. "You're not trying. You give in to these willful tempers. You're not yourself. I've got more than enough to do. You were never like this."

"Well, I am now. Simon beat Pippa for these."

"No wonder."

"He'd better have beaten me." Sara swung round, and Thomas was half touched by the horror in her. "She must have liked a book of mine," he said.

"They're in that wretched old-fashioned Plasticine," she went on, switching ground and speaking as if that compounded things. "Who could have given it to her? Prunella and I are so careful. She has plenty of the proper sort."

"This kind smells nice," he said.

"One of the *points* about the new kind is that it's odorless."

" 'Smell'!" he shouted. "Not 'odor.' You even take away smells. Actually, I think I probably gave her the clay."

"But we don't stock it."

"No, I got it from an art shop." In Sara's canon this was perfidy. She looked betrayed, and tight around the chin. "You'll have to put up with it, darling," he said gaily, refusing to fall in with her mood.

There was a pause while Sara collected herself, and then she said they must go back and do the accounts.

"I've got some work to do," he said.

"Yes, we have."

"No, my own work."

"In that case there are all the books to move."

"I'll go on with it here. There's more space."

"Have you asked Simon?"

"Why the hell should I ask Simon?"

A dam burst again: All he's done for you. (Prunella left the room.) Picking up the pieces of your life for you. A foreigner accepted as if you were his own father. No real son could have done more. Difficult times for everyone. Your trouble. Everyone under great strain. You didn't mean. The subject of Pippa better not discussed (and then discussed at length). It occurred to Thomas as he listened to her that Sara had not changed a whit in the whole time they had been married. No hint or taint of him had touched her. She had remained her strong English self, and in truth she did put up with a good deal, for in her terms a scholar's life must always have stood for a life of privation, which would explain the furious resolve that clenched the lines in her face. All the same, he had work to do.

"Before you leave, you'd better apologize to Simon," she said.

He left the room, picking up the little erotic figures and locking them into his desk drawer.

Sara followed him. "What are you doing?" she said.

"Nothing," he said.

"What are you thinking about?" She pursued him.

"Nothing," he said again, smiling at her, for she was Sara. ("Remember the nine tenets of resistance in a country occupied by foreign forces," he said to himself. "'We know nothing, we recognize nothing, we give nothing, we are capable of nothing, we understand nothing, we sell nothing, we help nothing, we reveal nothing, we forget nothing.'")

"Doesn't it hurt your pride? It must," she said, not unkindly but in a rare and urgent search for a response of any sort at all.

After contemplation, he replied quite seriously, "A little. Very little. At first. Not now. I think it's harder on you."

"You've never been properly recognized."

"You mean well paid." He waited. "To choose to do the work one wants, I suppose one will quite often have to renounce the idea of making a fortune. Yes? I'm sorry, my dear." A few minutes before, he had tried to add "We apologize for nothing" to the rules in his head, but he knew that Sara would always move him to compunction.

Alone then in his library, feeling fine, his spirits began to mount. He thought about some work, and also about the world, as he had not since he was in India. The sense of being part of a general flux had been lost for years. There grew in him a wish to touch with his fingers a future that he knew was that of many others. The disorder that had seemed to him for decades to determine the course of events regrouped itself like a pile of iron filings suddenly organized by a magnet, and he had a flash of optimism when it appeared quite possible that men in the days to come might wish to find out more than concerned them at the moment. Probably this curiosity will be quite superficial, he thought to himself, as it is in me until I have more time to spend on it. But it will be better. He considered for several hours, making notes and getting up now and then for books. He felt he had his hand on a way to proceed, and one that might be of some consequence, with luck. Simon's heavy tread moved about upstairs and his voice shouted something at a maid. He was calling for a sherry. "And a tonic water with ice for Mr. Flitch in the library. No gin. He doesn't drink. Remember that. Pru, he is still here, isn't he? He hasn't drifted back to his own place yet, eh? Do you think we have to offer him a meal?"

Thomas looked out of the window. I'll leap into my life, he thought, if it splits my face to bits.

As We Have Learnt from Freud, Therc Are No Jokes

➤➤➤ ➤➤➤ ➤➤➤ I married my Manhattan landlord. If I were a local, I suppose I would put that more delicately. But I come from Tobermory, a Scottish island village where it would not be such a craven blunder.

The beginnings with him were not auspicious, though.

I waited for him for an hour, outside his half-built apartment building. You could see him coming a block away. He wore a bright mustard suit. One of the Mafia? An evil-looking briefcase contributed. On the other hand, and leaving the suit aside, there was something pleasant about his stoop.

"Are you married?" he said at once, head turned toward the din from his workmen as he stepped past me over the rubble and put a key into the lock of the, I should have thought, not yet apt to be plundered building.

"I've been waiting an hour," I said. "The foreman promised you'd be here. I've got to find somewhere to live."

He scraped his shoes free of the mess outside, an act which interested, considering the dirt he was to step into. A piece of grit flew backward from his heel onto my eyeball. I had an impulse to say "Sorry," owing to my nationality, but managed to quench it.

"I'd like one of these apartments," I said.

He went in. "Married?" he said.

"No," I said, holding my eye. I suppose a New Yorker would have said "Yes," for prudence, but there wasn't much lust in the air.

"I can't have unmarried women," he said. "They're always getting raped on the way to the laundry."

As I left, with all speed, I noticed a sign outside the apartment building that said "Beware of the Dog." Rage weakened here, and I thought quite fondly of the workman within who must be in the habit of bringing some overloyal pet to the site.

The next day, after the thirty-third night spent on the exitless side of a bed that was shoved up against a wall and that also housed a physiotherapist called Daphne, an air hostess called Olga, and Olga's dopey Teddy bear, I got out of the bottom of the bed unheard and thought, *No.*

I rang the building site. The foreman said the owner was there.

"Can I speak to him?"

"He don't speak on the telephone."

So.

Do something else. Buy a birthday present for my grandmother on the way to work.

"I want a nightdress to send airmail," I said to a saleswoman in a fair-to-lousy cut-price shop. "For an old lady."

"This."

"No, something to the floor, I think."

"This."

"Haven't you got anything that goes to the floor?"

"This is waltz-length."

"She's eighty-one. I think she'd rather have something full-length.

"Everything is waltz-length or bikini. You want she should trip over and break her neck?"

So.

Push on to work. My employer, Simpson Aird, a friendly capitalist who calls me Miss Nib when he feels rumbustious, dictated letters in bed. His wife, Tessa, ate fried bread and tomatoes. Their six-month-old son was kicking on the bottom of the eiderdown. I picked him up while Mr. Aird thought. The baby treated me hospitably, being the age he is and therefore still inclined to interpret the rest of the world as an annex of himself. To be organic to somebody else's idea is an experience not to be sneezed at, in these divided times or any other. The Aird baby has a strong cast of thought and he imposes himself, philosophically speaking; as he stared at me, lying on my lap, he seemed like a hand of mine. Self and others. The usual tautology.

"How's the apartment hunt?" Mr. Aird said.

"Plugging on," I said.

"No luck?"

"Not yet."

Tessa said, "You'll suddenly find one."

"Or gradually," I said.

"You don't *gradually* find an apartment. You *suddenly* find an apartment," said Tessa.

"I might be inching up on it, mightn't I?"

"No," said Tessa, who sees things her own way as resolutely as any baby. "One day you'll simply have it, and then you won't remember what it was like to be without it."

"No?"

"You need some new clothes," said Tessa.

"Shall I get on with the letters?" I said.

Simpson peered at our two faces, scenting a row. Or a

wound. "My dear Miss Nib," he said, hurling himself out of bed and into the bathroom, "take a letter. I think you look first-rate." He imitated my Scots accent. "Furst-rate. Scrumptious." He sang "D' ye ken John Peel?" into the bathroom mirror.

So.

Revived, go back in the lunch hour to the apartment building, even if the landlord has twice more refused to come to the telephone. Swine.

He was standing in the foreman's office, looking troubled. Mustard jacket off; black pullover underneath. That stoop. A brooding and somewhat majestic effect. If swine, then big wild boar, hunting quietly in the woods for something, mooching about and turning things up.

The foreman was putting down the telephone. "They won't pay," he said to the landlord. "I told you."

"I've come about an apartment," I said. "I don't see why I have to be married. If it comes to getting raped on the way to the laundry, married women with a lot of washing must get raped more."

"Get them back on the phone," the landlord said to the foreman.

"You'll have to talk to them yourself," the foreman told him. "They're your insurers."

"No."

"You know what you've got, not talking on the telephone?" the foreman said. "You've got a hangup."

The landlord went on standing there, turned away from me.

"I want one of these apartments," I said to the foreman, who was drinking a Coke.

"Can't you see I'm busy?" he said.

"I've something on my mind," the landlord said softly to a concrete wall.

"What's happened?" I said.

"A *dog's* been stolen," the foreman said impatiently.

"Oh dear," I said. "Was it his?," looking at the large black back.

"It was to guard the plumbing," said the foreman, crushing the Coke tin with his hand and throwing it into a corner.

"What?" I said.

The landlord said, fast, "It was supposed to be guarding the plumbing, and if you think that's crazy then ask him about it. He told me to."

"It's you that's crazy," said the foreman. "What sort of a boss are you, doing what *I* say?"

"Trained to look after *plumbing?*" I said.

"These dogs are highly skilled," said the foreman.

"This one wasn't," the landlord said.

"Well," the foreman said, "what do you expect for eighty bucks a week? You got it cheap."

"It seems a heavy thing to steal, a bath," I said. "Let alone baths."

"I know it was only eighty bucks a week," the landlord said over me. "But eight *hundred* for the loss of the dog."

"You should've taken out insurance. You should've thought of that," said the foreman.

"Also, it was a nice dog," the landlord said, now sorrowing and private.

The foreman yelled something to the ceiling in another language and stomped toward the door saying, "The whole world is crazy, I tell you. Make your own telephone calls. What kind of a landlord are you, not speaking on the telephone?"

"You should've got the four-inch ducts finished on schedule," the landlord said. He took a couple of steps toward the man. "Then the plumbing would have been connected and we'd never have had to *have* your guard dog."

"Listen," said the foreman, swinging the door handle to and fro. The landlord had come to a halt. "I'm going to take time out to tell you something."

"Well, I pay for the time," the landlord defended himself, though not as intimidatingly as I could have hoped.

"One: Plumbing has to be bought in *ahead of schedule,* in case you lose a month's rent, O.K.? Two: The four-inch ducts were finished *last month.* It's the Mayor's *inspector* we're waiting on now. And why? Because you were too goddam mean to drop the five-hundred-buck payment to City Hall for *special services.*"

"Five-hundred-buck *bribe.*"

"*Payment.* For *special services,* for getting it *done.* See what happens when you waste your time in line?"

The foreman left. The landlord stood there. Now, to contradict myself, he didn't look like one of the Mafia at all. On the contrary.

"Shall we have some lunch?" he said.

"Yes, please. Could I have an apartment as well?"

He laughed. His eyebrows looked permanently as if they had just shot up. They had big half circles of pure white skin below. His hair was dark brown, and his face so asymmetrical that a reflection of it in a piece of broken mirror on the wall was unrecognizable. An exuberant man, nervous, poetic, with a way of pulling his long fingers one by one when something was making him laugh to himself. He was fun. I have never had such fun with anybody.

At our first lunch I asked for canneloni to fill myself up.

"Good. Girls are always thinning themselves," he said.

"What's your name, by the way?" I said.

"Murray Lancaster," he said. Pause. "Huh?" he said. "What are you looking like that for?"

"Well," I said, "I thought you were in the Mafia, but it's not much of a Mafia name."

"Why do you think I was in the Mafia?"

"Because you're a landlord, I suppose," I said, holding back the next thing I had been going to say and then deciding he might not mind. "Perhaps also because of your mustard suit."

He looked angry. It took me some time—weeks—to discover that he was poor and wore clothes handed on by a negligently competent brother-in-law in the soft-drinks business.

He asked my name.

"Emm," I said. "Emm McKechnie. My parents christened me Empyrean, but there had to be a way out."

"Do you believe that, in general?" he said.

"Yes, with luck," I said. He looked up fast, extremely pleased in a philanthropic way but still hanging back for himself. One could tell. Something more needed to be said, obviously. Wondering whether this was it, I told him I had a mustard suit, too. Ah, no. He concentrated on the menu. Hell, I thought. Patronage. The British abroad at their old work. But when I bent down on some pretext and could see into his face it seemed possible that he was laughing at himself as well as flustered.

Still with his head down, he ordered his own lunch. "A very rare steak," he said. And then, to me, "Vegetable?"

"Could I have a green salad?"

"And a very green salad," he said to the waiter before he could stop himself.

The foreman victimized him. Waiters made him feel a fool, this clever man. Spectres of poverty beset him, and he hankered after anything that would last. Perhaps that was why he had embarked, without capital, on trying to put up a building, though god knows this would have no long life in Manhattan. The little money he had saved was kept in seven different banks and also in his apartment, in the freezer locker of the fridge, inside a stringbeans packet. He made piles of quarters in his sock drawer when he emptied his pockets at night. After a few months, despite our best efforts, he went bankrupt and his knavish contractors were awarded all he had. We kept the loot that was in the freezer. We got married in a while. By then we were living in a dirt-cheap place on the Bowery. He hung on to his car. No bailiff would have touched it. He was deeply fond of it. It was a very old dark-green Hispano-Suiza, held together with beautiful leather straps like the ones my grandparents had on their steamer trunks.

He was a moving man, bashful but debonair. He was the only man I have ever known who once actually fell out of a hammock with laughing.

He slept on his back, at the edge of the bed by the telephone, near the door. I think he was frightened something would happen to us.

The following year he turned over in his sleep and crashed his leg onto my hipbone. It was like a piece of falling timber. Next morning I limped.

"What's happened?" he said from bed.

"You hit me with five ton of leg in your sleep. I didn't know a leg could be so heavy. It was like being socked with a Wellington boot full of mud."

"Should you go to a doctor?"

"Oh, no."

"What's a Wellington boot?"

"Gumboot. Rubber boot."

"I'm so sorry."

"I was rather pleased. It's the first time you've ever slept anywhere near the middle of the bed."

He groaned and looked away. "And the first time I do it I hurt you. I do things wrong too often. One of me is too many."

He thought of himself as a bungler. He thought he was infinitely dispensable and replaceable. From things he said in his sleep, I know he thought I was going to fall in love with somebody else. But we were allies. We were some sort of kin.

My husband died, my love, died in his car, on the night we put the clocks back, on the night of the extra hour that everyone else was glad of, though for my part I found no use to put it to. It was a Saturday night and I had a fortnight of holiday ahead of me while the Airds were unexpectedly away, not to speak of the obligatory Sunday to get through, the one that would have fallen to me in any case. I did what one does, moving myself about, reading the news, maintaining the circulation of the blood, for the accepted reasons. The heart and lungs carried on willy-nilly, keeping me going, keeping me awake. The need for sleep wasn't as merciful as it might have been. I would have to get my clothes cleaned, if I was to go on. I would have to telephone the grocer, if I was to go on. A pound of tea, I said; no, half a pound, thank you, and any bread that's got a European type of crust, and have you some Dundee marmalade? I don't like it here very much, not at the moment, I said, no doubt sounding like a dangerous recluse and a chauvinist to boot. Which would have been doubly misleading, for I had never felt more in search of company, nor indeed more indebted to Manhattan, the city without him being a great deal more like the city we had lived in together than anywhere else without him would have been. After a few days, nine or ten, I wondered if it would aid things to pay a visit to Scotland, but I hadn't the purpose for it, let alone the money. So I went and lived in public libraries and all-night cafés for a time. Someone moved me out, sooner or later, and it was probably just as well, for my attempts to find anyone to talk to had not prospered. "Do you think I could have a cup of tea, please?" I had said to a promising-looking man behind a counter, but it seems I should have said "Cup of tea" and left it at that, for he put his hands on his hips and shouted, "What's stopping you?"

When my holiday had the goodness to be over, I stood on the usual rush-hour bus and read a schoolboy's comic strips over his shoulder. There was sun outside. Life had several appearances of being on the mend. Halfway uptown, after a setback caused by a reminiscent cheekbone at the other end of the bus, I got a seat between a Chinaman and a Puerto Rican woman. I seemed to be taking up more than my share of the space, and the grief was bad again. I tried thinking of others, more as a device than a good, and clenched my thigh muscles for a start, to give half an inch more room to the neighbors.

"Excuse me," I said to the Chinaman. "My husband is dead."

The Chinaman grunted and dug his heel-shaped chin into his collar. It started to rain.

"Every morning this time the bus is full of nuts," the driver said with violence, not even visibly addressing me, though his right eye was glaring at me in his driving mirror. I spread my muscles again and took all the room I wanted. I should get my hair done, I thought. Widows slip if they let their hair go. Queen Victoria went downhill. It's a mistake to be wearing his watch.

"Hello," I said to the Puerto Rican child who was sitting on the lap of the woman beside me.

"Doan speak English," the mother said in the voice of a record, turning the child on her lap so that its back now faced me.

"Hi," said the Ukrainian doorman at the Airds' building, using the sum of the English that I had ever heard him speak, apart from "God bless," "Cab, sir?," and "You bet your ass." This morning he followed "Hi" with "How's life treats you?," so I thought he must have learned more English while I was away.

I said, "My husband's dead."

He laughed and said, "You bet your ass."

In the Airds' duplex apartment I hung my raincoat over Tessa's second mink with a malign hope that it would drip, which involved me in turning in my tracks after a minute or two to take the gesture back. The Chinese manservant caught me at it. I'm afraid nothing of the sort is hidden from him. There is no meanness he does not recognize. He winked in the direction of the Airds' bedroom and said, "Having late breakfast."

"Yes," I said coldly.

He winked again and said, "Nice holiday? Nice time with hubby?"

"My husband isn't well," I said, having no mind to hand him the truth at that moment.

The Airds were good to me. Cheerful. They made me move in to live with them as something they called their *au-pair* girl, mostly to exercise two new Great Dane puppies. The manservant, Wu, took me in hand in his own way and gave me makeup lessons. He sold cosmetics on commission. He had a fine and steady hand with an eyeline brush, like a miniaturist.

"You should go take Spanish at night school," he said one evening in the Airds' downstairs lavatory when we were clearing up after they had gone out to dine. He put one of their cocktail nuts into my mouth off a silver tray that he had balanced for the moment on the washbasin, and set himself to work on my mascara. "Meet Mr. Right," he said, twirling one of his makeup brushes in a half-empty glass of Simpson's after-office bourbon. Then the Airds came back for something they had forgotten. Wu panicked and locked the door.

One of the Airds tried to come in.

"Who's there?" said Simpson's voice.

Wu clapped his hand over my mouth and daftly said nothing himself.

"Who is it?" Simpson said again, firmly.

"It's only us," I said like a fool, through Wu's palm. Inapt. Wu and I were not us—not in any way.

The Great Danes slept in my room, unfortunately. I walked them for three or four hours a day, but nothing tired them or won their love. They seemed quite undevoted, except to each other. From an air hostess with a Teddy bear to two Great Dane pups. I lived in a room off the kitchen, so thin-walled that it was impossible not to hear what was happening in the dining room unless Wu had a gadget going. The garbage disposal, say, would drown things, but then it would stop and there I was, a living wiretap.

"We could send you our *au pair*," Tessa was saying one night. "She has a genius for sorting things out. You could pay her whatever you wanted."

"Can she really do filing?" said a woman's voice.

"She's Simpson's secretary," Tessa said. "She's got high speeds. She can even cope with the baby. She looks after the dogs at the moment to keep herself busy. She can do anything."

"It doesn't sound as if she's got much spare time."

"She doesn't know what to do with it. Her husband . . ."

Wu ran a beater for a short while. I had thoughts about the awesome hearings of eavesdroppers, of spies, of babies before memory. Then the beater was turned off, unmercifully.

"To tell you the truth, it'd be a relief to me if she did something adult. The dogs are too much of her life," Tessa said.

"She's a handsome girl," Simpson said. "She'll marry again. She's funny."

Tessa laughed gently. "Simpson worries about her. I think he's a bit in love with her." There was the sound of a kiss. Merriment.

". . . two defunct types of people now," the woman was saying. "Have you ever thought of that? It struck me the other day. The man of letters and the maiden aunt. Your *au pair* may be a born maiden aunt. From the sound of it, she's more like a relative to you than a servant."

"I don't think she wants to be a maiden aunt," Simpson said. "I don't get that feeling."

No, I thought. Though one can pretend, if required.

Some other day, Tessa came gaily into my room and pulled the dogs off the bed. "And what are you doing here, pray?" she said to them. "Emm doesn't want to see you today. It's Emm's day off." She kissed them.

"How can they tell it's my day off?" I said. "I'm here and they're here."

Tessa looked at me as if I had said something odd. "You should go out more," she said. "Take my charge plate and go shopping. How would you like to buy me a black cashmere sweater? No, that wouldn't be much of a holiday. Why don't you go and buy yourself a sweater, on me?"

"Or not?"

"That's something you say, isn't it? O.K., not, but for Christ's sake go out and enjoy yourself, my dear. You're sitting there like death warmed over."

It might be preferable, I thought, not to shop?

"She should get married again," I heard Tessa say to her mother-in-law on the telephone. "I'm going to send her to my doctor. She's got this thing about saying 'not' all the time."

So.

I went to her doctor. Tired to death, for some reason, and answering his questions in a doze.

"Perhaps you should get married again," he said.

"Why?"

"Sleeping all right?" he said, head down, plowing on.

"Who with?" I said, without thinking. Poor man.

"I meant, would you like some sleeping pills?"

"I'm fine. I don't need putting out. Do you think I should go and live in a commune in San Francisco? Somebody once asked me to. I wouldn't mind that."

"If you like the idea. Though people can get over-individuated in communes."

"Does that mean lonely?" I started to laugh.

He leaned forward. "Aha. Interesting. Now we have to ask ourselves why you're laughing, don't we? What you're avoiding." He shook his kindly head. "As we have learnt from Freud, there are no jokes."

So.

I coped with the amazingly uninteresting savories for one of the Airds' cocktail parties. I met a Bulgarian as I was handing round the cheese dip. He made some measure of pass at me. Given the circumstances of a cheese dip, it was cheering. However off the point.

Much later, I came back in to help Wu clear up the debris

and to take the puppies out for a walk. Simpson looked at me. At this tall, broad-shouldered girl. I tried to shrink. One of the puppies suddenly flung itself through the air and banged its wet nose against my right eye in its flight to a tray of vol-au-vent. Wu looked at me and gestured to his own right eye and giggled. He meant that my mascara had been licked off. "Brrr," I said, shaking my head and pretending to myself that I had dog's jowls. Any disguise to slink into, any animal mask.

"Perhaps you should go to an analyst," Tessa said. She put her arm around me. I laughed, and she said, "Laughing is a way of protecting yourself from the truth."

What? I thought, a laugh being pretty well the only dealing with the truth that offered itself at the moment, and so nothing to run down.

The Bulgarian took me out. I think he thought I was younger than I am. I think he thought I didn't recall anything about the war.

"I had to leave Bulgaria," he said. "You know where Bulgaria is?"

"Yes."

"You English girls are so educated."

"Scottish. But thank you."

"I had to leave," he said heavily, "because my conscience dictated that I inform on the Nazis."

"So you came here what year?"

"You have heard of the Nazis?"

"Yes."

"They were brutes. My conscience shouted that I had to inform. Bulgaria is a proud country."

"Bulgaria wasn't so proud in the war," I said. I thought about this, and then said, "I'm sorry," for he was a good-natured man. "I'm sorry. I've never even been there."

But he took no notice of either thing I had said, anyway, and laughed heartily at nothing evident about Sixth Avenue, and grabbed at my knee. "I do what I have to do, as they say in Western films," he declaimed, ogling my ear. "Bulgarians are masterly. In Bulgaria the woman is the man's slave."

"Are you hungry?" I said.

"Where shall we eat?"

"Where would you like?"

"When I take you out, you have to be my slave. You have to decide," he said, looking waggish, and also beginning to whine.

"What do you mean, your slave?"

"The man is superior."

"Oh," I said, glad of surrealism, though wondering who was to cope.

Silence unseated him. "What is it you do for the Airds, our friends?" he said desperately. "Apart from making succulent eats such as sardines?"

"I'm their nanny," I said. "To their Great Danes. Also their secretary, sometimes."

"So the Airds are Danish," he said. "Danish in ancestry. A proud race." He beat his chest and sang a song that turned out to be the old monarchist Bulgarian anthem.

"Slave," he said when it was over, "where shall we eat?"

"I like being mastered," I said, not sure how much money he had.

He looked suddenly suspicious that I was making fun of him, which I wasn't, and grabbed me to look down the front of my dress. "Aha. I spy a bra," he said. "I was thinking you were a member of Women's Liberation."

"I told you, I'm a sort of nanny."

"Women are inferior."

"Yes," I said. But now he looked inescapably furious, and

also seemed stalemated about what to say to the cabdriver. So I tried for a calming course, feeling thankful to this man for his dogged clasp on difficulties that wouldn't cause me any recall of my dead love in a million years, and I pursued the wisp of a path suggested by the word "nanny." "Women have babies," I said firmly to my redeeming friend, "so it's men who have to decide about spending money, such as money on restaurant bills."

"Bulgarian women have babies in hedges," he said, looking vaguely about him at the north end of Sixth Avenue.

I got him out at an ice-cream parlor after a while. I paid for the taxi because he had no change. We ate waffles. Perhaps he had no money whatever.

"You see," he said, maple syrup on his chin, "we are celebrating."

Celebrating, my fellow in farce, although neither of us belongs, to waffles or to one another. Of course, belonging may be gone by the board, historically speaking, she advises herself, wiping her face with this American paper dinner napkin and not wishing to be personal, to use a bygone phrase.

"What shall we celebrate?" I said.

"I give you a toast," he said, waving a doubled-over piece of waffle on his fork in salute. "To your beauty," he said, though my looks at the time were nothing to write home about, "coupled with the birthday of the King of Bulgaria."

"The ex-King?" I said, which was hurtful, so I toasted the man in coffee. "His Majesty," I said. "Will he be having a party?"

"We have sent him a loyal birthday telegram in exile," he said. "My name is at the head of the list. Boris Blagov, chairman."

"Chairman?" Now I knew his name.

The heartening nature of repetitions. Obviously fortified by my inane echoing, Boris clutched my knee. "I am the leader of the forty-five members of the Bulgarian Monarchist Front," he said.

"Forty-*five?*" I said. It seemed best.

"After our celebration I shall take you to a solemn service," he said, gripping my left ankle between his shoes. At the same time he looked at his watch. We left in haste. He took me to a church where the other forty-four members of the Bulgarian Monarchist Front were mustered outside the front doors. All entrances were locked.

"I myself shall get the keys," Boris said to me stylishly. "Because I am the leader. The keys are in New Jersey."

We took a cab to New Jersey and back. I paid. We went through the service at two in the morning. Some of it was very fine. The priests were out of voice through tiredness. At three, Boris took me home. He tiptoed from the elevator to the apartment door with erotic wheezes.

"I cannot lovemake to you," he said at the door, "in the house of our ancient Danish friends where you are the nanny."

"Never mind," I said.

But he came in all the same, not apparently wounded. He wanted a drink. The Airds had long since gone to bed. I felt no right to sit in their drawing room but no call to take Boris to my bedroom. So we went to the dining room. He dived gaily at my legs, like a football player. I thanked him in my head for so thoroughly putting paid to the past, at least for the moment. One of the Great Danes was simultaneously clambering into my lap, trying to get all four legs fitted into the available footage, under the delusion that she was some other size. It is a delusion that many of us have, including Boris and possibly myself.

"How I am jealous of the young puppy in your lap," Boris said.

Liar, I thought, and so feeling a trifle low but at the same time in his debt. By half past five he had drifted off to sleep underneath three paws of the other dog, which had taken to him. He had been muttering vows of romantic love, rather sullen. He slipped into Bulgarian and became not absurd. Other people, alive and kicking. Other people to blot out a face.

I went to sleep near him, on the floor.

Tessa came in at half past eight and looked overjoyed. She drew me into the kitchen and stretched out her arms, leaning backward a bit, and said, "How I love people who say 'Yes' to life." Then she asked why I was laughing again, and I said that that wasn't what had happened, and she looked angry, and I had a shower. I don't like showers, but the bathroom was the only place in the apartment where I could lock a door on myself. I wondered why the best-off nation in the world should have chosen showers instead of baths. Dreams of childhood garden sprinklers, perhaps. I sat on the step of the shower and went to sleep and then wept. The voice of the dead rang in my ear. "Say 'No.'" The only time I cry now is in my sleep.

Days later, when I had decided to find myself a less cushy job, someone telephoned me and said, "You are ruining my life."

"Who is it?" I asked, unforgivably.

"So soon you forget a passion," said Boris.

Apologize. Explain. Say "How are you?"

Boris moaned. Silence.

"Thank you for the other night," I said.

"I am a wreck," he said. "You are making me a wreck."

"Why? Oh dear." Again, silence. I said, "Boris, I didn't mean why; I meant how? How am I making you a wreck?"

"You force me to sleep with a Great Dane puppy. I am a

proud man." I started to laugh, but I don't believe he heard. "A Great Dane puppy. I am a Bulgarian," he said.

"I'm sorry. You'd dozed off," I said.

"My life is ruined. I have laid my life at your legs and yet you say nothing. What can I do to get you off the phone?"

"Should I ring off?"

"I'll kill myself if you ring off."

I looked at my watch. "Could you get yourself some lunch?" I said. "Treat yourself to a *nice* lunch, and go to bed? Could you?"

"I'd choke," he said, putting the receiver down. He rang back again at once and mistakenly carried on with the Airds' answering service, not realizing that the woman there had picked up by the time I got to the phone.

"You English girls are so cruel," he was saying.

The answering service said, "One moment, please."

"I'm here," I said. "It's me. I was getting your number from Tessa."

"You are ruining my life, I tell you."

"Could I take you out to lunch?"

"You ruin my life all by one little word."

"Which little word?"

"The most terrible word in your cruel language," he said, putting the phone down.

He rang back several times to say that the word was "no." Twice he had his mouth full. Once he said it to the answering service.

Tessa grew testy about the line's being used all the time, and said that the Bulgarians were the worst lovers in the Balkans, as though that were a world-known fact, like the trying nature to others of our gentle Scottish weather. I was laughing, which was the debt I owed him. But what if he wasn't faking? What if he wasn't funny?

The Last to Go

➤➤➤-➤➤➤-➤➤➤ "Get out," said Stephen Brandt's best friend. "And shut up."

"I am out," Stephen said, not moving from his best friend's own armchair in Dulwich. "To all intents and purposes. And I'm effectively shut up because I've been kicked out of my job and also because you don't seem to have heard a word I've been saying." He tried to leave the chair and go, but didn't badly enough want to, and carried on with a furious daydream of what the trades-union movement might come to represent again in England, although England was only half his country.

The best friend, Felix—an affectionate, forgetful, hypomanic man passionately expert in animal physiology and the history of Communism—yelled benignly at his wife for more coffee and said again, "Get out. You're boring when you're like this. Go and talk to somebody from the library."

"There is no more library. I've been sacked."

" 'Jesus wept.' "

"What?"

"It's the shortest verse in the Bible."

"I know that. There is no more Bible."

"You're really down, aren't you?" said Felix's wife, who had come in with a jar of instant coffee and a jug of water no more than fairly hot, which increased Stephen's worry that many things were falling behind. He had memories of Vienna before the 1939 war, and liked people who took care over such things as coffee—proper, expensive coffee—as he tried to himself, however much he decided to ignore most of the facts of being poor.

"Not altogether down," he said.

"He's just caught Socialism," said Felix.

"All over again," Stephen said. "I didn't think you could get it a second time. I can't imagine why, when the Labour Party's such a swindle. It must have been Czechoslovakia. That possibility."

"Probably chemical," Felix said. "I've known of chemical conversions to ideology."

"It's more like love," Stephen said seriously. "You never think you can get that twice."

Felix pondered a bad time that Stephen had had with a girl a while ago, and fiddled with his shortwave radio. It was believed by the other people in his street, the owners of the other semi-detached red-brick villas with Victorian stained glass over the front doors and children's tricycles in the halls, that Felix was a Communist spy. His absorption with Mao and Castro was so open that the neighbors took it for a double bluff, and each new discovery of an agent transmitting messages from some ordinary-looking English suburb increased the tension of their interest in the land mine who was surely bound one day to go off in their own street. Stephen knew of the rumor and had neither evidence nor time for it. He had been Felix's friend since 1938. They were young Communists together after Stephen fled Austria. His father, now dead, had been an English book translator living in Vienna. His mother, also dead, was really German, but she had called herself Austrian in an impulse of cowardice that Stephen rather cherished her for. The times had made him mistrust the militant kinds of heroism, though he unjustly saw himself as deficient in fortitude of another sort. He had been born with a curved spine and stood five feet.

"What are you going to live on?" said Felix's wife.

"I don't need much."

"And what are you going to do?"

"I'm going to resign from the Labour Party to make my position clear, and then I don't know."

Even Felix refrained from asking him who would notice.

Felix's wife started talking about poetry, which she wrote, while Felix shouted about his last visit to Castro. Stephen listened carefully to both, his head forward and down, like a horse's hanging over a gate, which was a way he had and not altogether due to the curve in his spine.

"I thought I might go to America and help the anti-draft students around the Army camps," he said.

Felix's wife began to recite her poetry, and wondered about his air fare, and gave him some coffee. Felix thought of Czechoslovakia and then careered into a fantasy of Ho Chi Minh gossiping about the minor members of the English Royal Family. He started to shout again.

"Though perhaps one should try to do something to rescue Socialism here," Stephen said softly, through both of them. "I thought I might go and talk in factories."

"You're out of your mind!" Felix yelled. "England's as dead as a doornail. Greedy. Dozy. Worse than America. The whole system has to be changed."

"Sh-h-h," said Felix's wife.

"Why?" said Felix.

"There's a nice worried American on the run from the draft next door."

"Well, I said we were even worse, didn't I?" Felix glared at her.

"Then why do you like it here?" Stephen said. "You love England as much as anyone I know."

"It's the only possible place to live," Felix said, putting on a record of North Vietnamese songs with the volume up very loud.

Stephen made a few moderate reservations about England in his own soft voice, which was audible over the hubbub like some supersonic protest. Felix's wife went on stoutly reading her poetry as if she were not shy, roaring to keep the beat against the Vietnamese and walking round and round the dining table in time with herself.

"What *do* you like about England?" Stephen said again.

"It's *mellow,* Stephen!" Felix bawled angrily, on his feet, with his arms swinging on a curve away from his body and looking abnormally long. "MELLOW!" he shouted, louder still. Stephen laughed, and Felix felt vaguely resentful, but it was fine at the moment to see his friend laughing, even at his expense, so he brushed the mood away and continued with an invention about Mao studying Princess Anne's record at gymkhanas. He appeared to be airborne, but he was watching Stephen out of the corner of his eye.

"I'm going home," Stephen said, and no one asked where that was. He had just been booted out of his digs, for the nth time, because the landlady had complained about the noise of a child who had stayed with him on the way home for half-term. But presumably he had a place to go, and he would prefer to keep that problem to himself.

"He looks minute," Felix's wife said, watching him from their gate as he marched down the road to the bus stop.

"He could never stand up and lecture for weeks on end in all those factories." Felix remembered the gang of them at the beginning of the World War, with Stephen stomping around reviling the call-up, deciding on conscientious objection for himself, shaking off the hand of any acquaintance who tried to help him speed over a dangerous crossing, and talking about the anti-militarist statement he would make to the court. None of his friends could possibly have pointed out that there was no question of his ever passing the physical.

"Men are very fragile," Felix's wife said, looking at her giant husband, who was standing under a street lamp stirring his arms like propellers.

"I'm going for a walk, dear," he said, absently. He always went for a walk about this hour. And then he got up again at half past five to read.

"I wish we needed the same number of hours' sleep," she said. "I wish we went to bed at the same time. I always fall off while I'm waiting for you."

"I liked the coffee tonight," he said, not allowing that it was the same instant coffee as ever, and to deserve the goodness she determined to go up to Soho tomorrow for some beautiful fresh espresso beans.

Then she swore out of the blue and said, "The truth is, you know, I suddenly hope Stephen doesn't come again. Not unless he's more manageable. He's upsetting. I hate just anyone dropping in. I can't stand it."

"He's not just anyone. He's Stephen."

"Those terrifying high hopes. What's he going to do with them? Did his back look worse to you?"

As happened in their life together, Felix was humbled for a flash by a sense that she had caught something he had missed: something wild in the air Stephen had brought with him. "Come on, old girl," he shouted, "calm down!" and later he found her a scientific paper to read, which she liked.

"Here," said Stephen Brandt to life, walking down the Strand at eleven o'clock the next dampish morning and moving his lips without a sound. "You think I've had enough. Well, I haven't, not by a long chalk, and I'm not the tramp I look, either. It's a bad time, admitted, there's truth in that, but I shouldn't choose to be out of it. A lax and, O.K., a dishonorable time. Immigration Act, Rhodesia, Gomulka, Prague, America having a national nervous breakdown, the soul of England on the ropy side. Hope in the students, as long as you don't get too utopian about it and start to laugh. Expect nothing. That's the trick. Conceive of the boundless, but expect nothing whatever. There won't be an apocalypse from English students, not from that quarter, I shouldn't suppose. Though who can tell? Stupidity of trying to conclude. In the sense of reaching any conclusions. Also, of course, in the sense of ending. I have never been further from suicide in my life, though I imagine my friends would find it quite opportune. Understandably. My lack of means is extreme, granted, and I look bad, skin white, mouth chapped, body apparently even shorter than usual, eye roaming and I daresay a bit fretful, trousers in bad shape, attention astray for a book lying around to pinch or even an old magazine, since I sold a few volumes I should now like to have kept, in exchange for a slug of what turned out to be the world's nastiest though cheapest whiskey. A poor impulse. I ordered a quadruple. Something I've never done before or since in my life. It was very necessary, and it made a sunny improvement in the event. So one looks forward."

"Listen," Stephen said to a woman at Labour Party headquarters in Transport House. "I've come to resign."

After a pause, while she knitted and changed to a new ball of wool, she surprisingly said, "Oh dear."

"That's nice of you," he said, blood having started to boil.

"No call to be formal about it," she said. "If you feel like re-signing, all you have to do is let your dues lapse. I don't sup-pose they're paid up anyway. They never are."

"Mine are."

"Don't you be so sure. Bertrand Russell's weren't and a nice pickle he got himself into, though I'd put it all down to that secretary if I were asked. Speaking personally."

"Anyway, I want to hand in my card. I want my position to be clear. I've written a letter to my Member of Parliament, but I want it to be clear at headquarters."

"What?"

"That Socialism in England has turned out to be a bitter farce." He looked at her knitting, which continued, approach-ing the heel of the sock in progress, and wondered if she was ever going to glance at his card on the counter.

"And who am I supposed to send it to, may I ask?" She banged down her knitting. "I can't read the signature." With distaste: "You're not famous or something, are you?"

"No."

"I can't do anything with the matter if you won't give me the details. No skin off my nose."

He stayed silent. Chin not more than four inches above the sill of her cubicle. She stood to get a pencil. Five feet seven, eight.

"Stephen Brandt, is it?" she said. "It seems to be paid up."

"Since 1940."

"It's a meaningless gesture, you know. Handing it in." She spoke coldly, and he hated her, and the height of her, and of a man behind her. The tall, those engrossers of manhood, those hyperbolic exemplifiers of the species, the monsters who over-look us.

"There's no such thing as a meaningless gesture," he said, after emptying himself of that thought. "If it *is* a gesture, then it must always have a meaning."

"Well." She sniffed, and considered. "There's an interesting idea," she said, throwing him into next week with the surprise of it. People change, he told himself. I might remember not to treat people as if they could only act in one way. I suppose they could always act differently.

"Are you turning Tory? That's all they're going to want to know," she said.

"No." He thought, Is that really all they'll want to know? And proceeded to plan a call on some of his old Communist Party mates during his walk back home.

"It's odd that I haven't heard of you. You're sure you're not a celebrity masquerading?" She looked at his clothes with disbelief and a little pity. "Otherwise I don't know why you've come. I mean, you're not a nut."

"No?"

"We've experience in recognizing nuts in this place."

Well, he thought, she said I'm not a nut. One can reckon that to be all to the good, from a stranger. To be plain, I'm a bit exhausted, secretly, about the intellectual advantages that are supposed (by intellectuals) to accrue from being physically underendowed or peculiar-looking, though it's possible to keep up the front in public and many a gulled beloved has supposed that this joke of a frame is where my energy comes from. (*What energy?*) Hellfire to, for instance, Annabel, for her loving farewell about "understanding the beleaguered ferocity of the uncommon." Silly bird. Too much upbringing can mess a person about. She meant she was frightened, didn't she? She said I was too much for her, and I assume she thought she was being admiring, though she certainly meant I was not enough. Boiling oil on the head of her. Where is she now? On the right side, of course, doing her best about Vietnam, et cetera. And not betraying the past, either, not rewriting our private history to suit herself. That isn't her flaw at all. She said she wanted to go to Peking. With her children. Ye gods, I said, with the babies? There are crèches in China, she said. Well, yes, I know that, O.K., I said, you're their mother, and you decided against their father for reasons I take to be desolate, but wouldn't some Asian studies in St. James's Square at the Institute of International Affairs be less perilous until they are both over, say, four? And then she quite confounded me by doing exactly what I advised, and I always thought she took me for a crank whose horse sense, if any, was a forced calm not to be heeded. And when the babies were both a ripe four-plus, and she did indeed go off to Peking and left them with me, the ensuing fun made me wonder sometimes whether I was their father, which is no question to put, since the answer should be proffered, I suppose. I should like to have been a parent, a real English Socialist, a stunning diver on the side, and a foppish dresser. Just look at these clothes. I wish I were an orator. Or a political writer of great eloquence. I should like to speak to people of their other lives.

Then Brandt went into a tea shop, in spite of feeling that his new landlady's fried bread for breakfast was going to be more than enough to see him through the day. Food lay like clods of clay in his stomach and it rained, but he was supported by a sense of majesty in ideas and even in himself for having them, though this latter maintenance came and went. He thought of a Socialist future for his half country, and conceived the hope of a job in which he might have the luck to be gripped by some stupendous ire of work, trying to avoid the spectacle of the people around him and in the wet street outside, which pointed out a fraternal indifference in the world that was the last perception he cared to harbor. It was a time when he was immensely drawn to panache, and he felt done with the prim and the hangdog for good. He suddenly saw Annabel passing in the street outside. It was a year or more since they had met, but he ran out of the shop and clung to her elbow. They ran ill-assortedly up the street in the drizzle. She was the taller and also he ran with difficulty, but she was used to the coupling and minded nothing. They talked as they ran, and he was elated. They made plans to spend the day together. He experienced a considerable longing for a whole life of shambles and baked beans.

They started for a Communist Party hangout. He warned her, and himself, that the call was likely to be a waste of spirit. All the same, he dearly hoped that the mood there might match his own. He felt like the man in an old music-hall joke who hammers on the dentist's door with a wet sponge, the need to get in conflicting powerfully with the longing to flee.

As it turned out, of course, the people in the seedy upstairs room couldn't provide any of the raw exuberance he wanted. At the same time, he was much too committed to them by years in common for their limp urbanity to strike him as funny in world-changers. What they expressed was not so much any possibility of revolution as a sort of chivalrous exasperation at things as they would always be. He introduced Annabel and told the watchful, exhausted-looking ring of people that she was working at night with a set of young Left Wingers who published a broadsheet the old guard knew all too well. It was immediately clear that he had put his foot in it. While an angry woman in a cardigan sadly toasted herself a crumpet by the jet of a gas fire, he tried to shift to another topic. He said he was thinking of going to America for a while. He also said, rashly, that he felt stirred by the efforts of American radicals.

This turned out to be essentially the same menacing subject as the earlier one.

"Riot guides and drug protests and minor jokes about policemen," said a man in a mackintosh, standing up by the gas fire and talking fixedly about the broadsheet, eying it in its filing place. "They don't know the power of what they're up against. They won't define it. They pinch most of what they say from the student press in America and throw in a few tags from Colonel Ojukwu. Never enough to be serious. That's the thing, they're simply not very substantial."

"They suggested putting marbles under the hoofs of police horses," said the woman with the crumpet.

"She's not being sentimental," the man in the mackintosh said. "*Any* measures would be permissible if there were a structure of thought behind them."

"They don't know any history," the woman said. "They don't even know anything about the war. I sometimes think they have a neurosis about not having been in the blitz."

Feeling hampered, Stephen managed to plow on with a story about a Yale graduate who was in prison for fighting the Vietnam draft.

"There's no weight to isolated acts of self-aggrandizing heroism in a decaying society," said a man who was generally nice, and who bore on his forehead the triangular scar of a marble paperweight that had been thrown at him by his best friend, a Tory, for a sentence like that.

"Self-aggrandizing?" said Stephen, rising to the bait when he knew better. "He's in prison."

"Well, he's celebrity-seeking enough to have made you talk about him."

"Scarcely anyone has heard his *name*. You hadn't. I asked him once why I'd never seen him mentioned in any of the endless stuff about his movement, and he said he thought some of them had to stay anonymous. 'Look at the famous ones,' he said. 'They can't move. They're pinned. We have to have spokesmen, but we also have to leave some of us free to do things,' he said."

"What's special about that?" asked the woman by the gas fire.

"I just thought it was rather remarkable in a boy of twenty-three. It seemed grown-up," said Stephen.

"It's all by the way," said a thin man impatiently from behind his desk, which was stacked with political magazines. There was a photograph in the chaos. His wife in their garden. He had a collection of little ivory animals on his pencil tray. He arranged them in a Noah row as he talked. Stephen found it impossible not to be fond of him. "There's no program," the man said frantically, putting a bear behind a hippopotamus. "It's the vice of America to believe in the random."

"No, I don't think so," Annabel said suddenly, and then stopped.

"Go on," Stephen said to her.

"It's only that I think, maybe, that it's more the vice of America—no, not vice, I don't think, but difficulty—to be moralistic in politics. Is that right?"

The man behind the desk paused and said, "It's a point," with no interest at all.

Annabel dried up entirely.

"Haven't a clue what that signifies," said the woman by the fire, speaking through the crumpet. "Would anyone like the other half of my crumpet? Speak up or I'll have wolfed it."

"Have you got a boy friend working with that lot?" the scarred man asked Annabel with a pounce.

"No," Stephen said, stabbed, just realizing that she had. He stood up and walked to the window of the cold, cold room, putting aside with contempt his lifelong habit of arranging to be seated so as to hide his size when he was about to say anything that interested him. "The trait she's talking about. It's a confusion. It gives a moral force that's spurious . . . that's troubling to America . . . a moral force to political crimes, for instance." He looked around and saw a great many faces all wearing the same expression, an expression stating that they were never going to be surprised by anything in history and that they had already had every thought that was ever going to be in his head. "I think she means it's a hard, an exacting connection to make," he pushed on, "this connection between moral behavior and political behavior. . . . With a moral question, you ask yourself whether you can go on living as yourself if you do such and such a thing. But that isn't politics. It's self-conservation." The woman made a pile of cracked Minton tea plates in the wire in-tray that she used for stacking the washing-up. "It doesn't *work* very well as politics. Though you're bound to try to make it work, I do see," he said, watching her hands, "in a place where opportunism's gone mad and grown so repulsive as a political dynamic."

"Blimey," said Annabel. "Anyway, when wasn't it repulsive?"

"I hadn't finished." He looked at her face and tried harder to speak for her. To her, perhaps. "People before us . . . Other times accepted it. They always found it natural in government. Opportunism was what kept politics going. America may be . . . It's the suicidal greatness of America, I think Annabel means, to have raised opportunism to such a point that even people who wouldn't dream of ditching anything else feel that this has to be plucked out. Which is politically much like trying to run your old car without petrol."

"I *suppose* that was what I meant," said Annabel.

He took her away. "What is it?" he said. "I hated what I was saying, too."

"You undercut too much."

"There's no need to listen to me. Even I don't, altogether."

"Yes, you do. You're in a bad way, aren't you? You don't know what next."

"Spit in the face of the century?" he said.

"I'm frozen," she said. "What's the poor century done?"

He blew nearly a pound on a taxi to get them home in comfort, and she seemed glad to hold his hand. "It's very nice to see you," he said. "Are you all right?" He meant, among other things, are you living with anyone? and she knew it, but she cared too much for the day together to tell him one way or the other.

"Where are the children?" he said. "You haven't sent them to boarding school?"

"Are you out of your mind?" she said. "I usually have one under each arm."

"Where were you going? I forgot to ask."

"I need some tights," she said. He stopped the taxi at a shop and they bought tights at speed while the meter ticked.

"Could I see them? The kids?" he said when they had got back to his digs.

"Yes. Shall we have something to eat? Have you got any baked beans?" she said, to his joy. The tins were hidden behind a shelf of books because his landlady forbade cooking in the room, apart from kettle-boiling. "You nit," Annabel said. "Behind the books is the first place she'll hunt." They ate with a shared teaspoon out of the tin and she looked at the sardines and condensed milk now exposed between John Donne and Rosa Luxemburg.

"What?" Stephen said, worried.

"It's like tea caddies. All burglars know that ninety-eight per cent of all housewives decide to hide things in the tea caddy." Stephen was felled by the things she knew. She passed him the tin and the spoon, and lay on the floor looking at the gas fire, and then she went to sleep. I was here once, he thought, stirred by a recollection that was not at all like an ordinary memory but more like a flash of *déjà vu* about some great happiness known before he was born. "This is what it was like," he said to himself. "I have been here."

When she woke, he was looking at the fire and reading P. G. Wodehouse.

"What are you thinking about?" she said.

"Wodehouse," he said.

"What else?"

"Food. Loot, you, and also me. And also what to do."

"In what way?"

He kept quiet. He had been wondering where political allies might be, if anywhere. He suddenly saw that she was crying, though she said it was because of looking at the fire.

"Wouldn't you like to go and get the children and come to stay here for a night or two?" he said. "We could fit in somehow."

"The landlady would have an attack."

"I'd like it very much." He paused. "I could tell her I'd sleep in the bathroom." He paused again. "I could even *really* sleep in the bathroom, if you like."

"Is it your own? Don't you share it?"

"The other bed-sitter's empty."

"And she wouldn't let you sleep *there* overnight? No, I suppose not, old cow. Is she a cow, this one?"

"No."

Annabel held her head. "Darling, what am I blathering about? It's quite unrealistic to think of. I've got to go to a meeting. I should have been back at the office. It was my *lunch hour*. It's half past four."

"Not worth going back," Stephen said cheerfully. "Will you get the sack?"

"No. I might have to sack myself. It's that sort of place. Oneself and one's conscience and the filing cabinets. You're put on trust, like a spaniel."

A little later, she said, "Come to the meeting with me. You might feel at home, I think. And then I honestly will have to go away."

He felt her eluding him and said, "What are you hiding?"

"I'm in love with someone. You obviously knew that, though. I'm living with him, on and off. Mostly on, with luck. Called Charlie. You'll meet him if you come this evening. You'd like him."

He was irritated by a piece of smut on her cheek and started to wipe it off, and then pretended he had been stroking her, because he saw her distress at an emotion that she had guessed with her usual impossible correctness. He took her to her meeting. She told him on the bus, nerving herself, that the children were Charlie's but that she had undertaken of her own accord not to tell anyone else because Charlie was the sort of person who couldn't be lumbered.

"Lumbered?" Stephen said only. Wait, breathe, start again.

"He's always going away. I suppose he has to. Does he? The thing is, I never believe he's going to come back. I couldn't tell anyone else this. It's not painful to hear, is it? My dear friend."

"That's the trouble with women and dogs," Stephen said furiously, heart splitting for a second, because it was also the trouble with himself, now and then. "They never believe you're going to come back. They don't know the meaning of soon."

"Isn't the same thing true of you?" she said. "Of men?"

"I'm not a man, I'm a phenomenon," he said, with no expression.

"Who isn't?" she managed. She heard that he was speaking wretchedly, not arrogantly, but it would have been a patronage to recognize that any further, and she had to let him be rancorous.

The meeting was in a Notting Hill flat. The room was full of young men talking politics and being affably rude to each other. They wore clothes that he thought beautiful, when he could see for envy: jackets with Napoleonic pockets, trousers cut so that they reached the ground at the back, pink shirts, print ties. There were a few girls there. One of the young men had been hurt in a demonstration and his clothes were spattered with his blood. He was holding his left eye. His girl leaned over him, talking to him, with her long straight hair swinging over his face. In a corner of the room there was a mimeograph machine. A girl and a man were working it, faces transparent from fatigue. Cheery posters hung on the wall, and there were a lot of tables shaped like children's bricks that did for stools or in-trays, made of clear Perspex and spotted with dabs of red and blue paint. Annabel tried to persuade Stephen to join her on a bright-blue canvas swing seat with Charlie. Stephen had already taken in two things: that he was with a set of people he would have liked very much to belong to, and that Annabel was hitched to a man who treated her idly. The two observations did not go well with each other. Like most strong men in an extreme of daze and hurt, he spoke many unnecessary words. One or two of the people he spoke to found him politically fascinating, even if they did take his style of callous irony with no irony of their own. They spoke of him later rather generously. Stephen left as soon as possible, maintaining brusqueness.

He had a cup of tea with his landlady before he went to bed. Felix had tracked him down through his old address and left a note. That cheered him. The landlady, Mrs. Jenkins, was married to a fifty-five-year-old man who drove a vegetable lorry. He kept dropping off in their presence because he went to work at three every morning.

"This is a country that should export," Mrs. Jenkins said. "We always seem to be importing and I don't know why. We'll be devalued again and any fool but the government can see it coming, can't they? Alfred, you shouldn't eat that."

"Why not?" said Mr. Jenkins, wide awake with the cheek of it and now taking not one but two pieces of her best fruitcake.

"The doctor says it's harmful to you."

"Doctors have been the cause of many people dying."

"Well, Mr. Brandt," said Mrs. Jenkins, turning, "I don't know what your politics are, but we're old trades-union people and I'm disappointed. We should export more, as I was saying. That's what all the papers keep telling them and yet none of them take a blind bit of notice. Governments are paid to know things like that. To think quicker than us. It's not our job, after all. Yet it seems they keep doing the wrong thing at the wrong time, according to the papers. It'd make me pack it in and go to Canada if I was younger, but you can't leave England, can you?" She poured some more tea. "This monkeying around. It's bad for the country. It's a worry, isn't it?"

"I'm half Viennese, you know. I'm only half English."

"But you've always lived here." She adjusted to something hopeful.

"Since I was eighteen. I usually call myself half German because people get so fed up with all the Germans who say they're Austrian."

"Well, I don't suppose it was easy, the war, wherever you were. Mr. Jenkins and I had a very nice friend who came from Italy. He spoke perfect English, like yourself."

Stephen read for hours upstairs. People manage on short

commons, he thought in the middle of his book. He dreamed of the bloodied face with the girl's hair swinging over it, and of Annabel's children, and then he surfaced again and went for a walk through Covent Garden fruit market, where Mr. Jenkins must already be at work. There was the usual fine smell from the apples spilled and crushed in the gutter. He contemplated eating a meat pie at the stall by the church, but he had enough experience of phantom hunger at night to know that it would disappear of its own accord by morning and that it was best not to squander money on appeasing it. He went to bed and dreamed again. Two old-age pensioners were dancing in a ballroom lit by chandeliers. They were jostled by smart young people, and no one would do anything for them. It's the bad hour of the night, he thought, awake. Mrs. Jenkins seemed to be in the room, looking sad. Excuse me, he thought, addressing himself to her, excuse me if I'm being personal, but when was your last laugh? Not long ago, she said in his head, one comes to rely on one's bit of fun, and he tried her with a joke or two, but the old happy creasing of the face took a time to occur. Then Annabel, actual Annabel, broke into the night by throwing gravel up at his window to attract his attention. She looked strange. She had the children with her. It seemed that she had had a row with her man and that he had left.

"For good?"

"More or less. It's always more or less. This time I made it happen, I think." Her voice was blurred.

The children were jolly enough. They trundled about the room looking at things and then sat behind one another on his bed and played train carriages.

"They should be asleep, shouldn't they?" Stephen said, and the five-year-old said, "No, of course not, it's today now."

"They'll never go off now that it's light. I'm going to be

sick." Annabel staggered out of the door and he followed her. She sat on the rim of the bath and then fell onto the floor. She wouldn't speak or open her eyes, and he shook her very hard.

"I was asleep," she said thickly.

"Are you drunk?"

"I've taken sleeping pills. Only two. I only wanted to go to sleep." She started to get hysterical and self-pitying. "I've run out of money and I'm trapped with the children and I don't like it here. It's a bad time."

"Don't gripe. Change it."

"You've got energy. You're remarkable. It's different for you."

"Change it."

She opened her eyes and glared at him. "All very well to say. You don't know what it's like."

"No?"

"Don't be sarcastic. I didn't mean you've got much, except this energy. I only meant you're more used to it." The children shouted next door and Annabel covered her ears and said, "I can't."

"That's not true of yourself."

"I just can't. I want to go to sleep for a month. I don't like any of it. I hate my rotten job and I'm still not earning enough and I don't see the kids enough and there aren't enough people like you with enough of whatever it is to change anything. None of it's enough." She went to sleep, and woke to growl, "Me least," and he put a bath towel round her and tried to carry her into his bed-sitting room, but he was too frail to do it and she had to wake up again to walk by herself. She opened one eye and grinned at him. The children were playing the Wurlitzer on his typewriter and chatting to each other. It seemed such a good morning in many ways that he was prompted to an unbearable hope and said, "Would you ever marry me?"

"Perhaps I could stay here for a day or two," she said. But she had to reply. "I'm a tramp. Both kinds. Tramps shouldn't marry. I'm not in love with you." There was another pause, and then she said, "Maybe," which he knew for no.

She went to sleep for a respite, and when she woke up Stephen was in drafty self-possession. He was holding one of the children, who was asleep. "Look," he said, trying to help her. "You're born nobody and on your own. So you've nothing to lose, have you? It's not a bad position to strike from."

The Position of the Planets

>>>>>>>>>>> "Good lord, I'm a genius," the impresario wailed, as if crying for help. He held his hand to his forehead and loped across the bar toward the beautiful girl in the corner. "I'm a *genius*," he said again, and the hand again went to his forehead. He might have been taking his temperature. "I dreamt about you suddenly last night, and now here you are in New York of all places. You won't remember me."

"Nearly," the girl said, trying. Also still trying to write a letter.

"Well, it's a great piece of luck, to break a dream. I've been having wonderful luck ever since May 25th. I'm Scorpio. In the dream you were in London, of course. What are you doing here? We were both in London. We were in the National Theatre bar, the downstairs bar, the place where I last saw you. You won't remember. Can I sit down with you and have a drink?" He loomed over the table and spilled a pile of show-business newspapers from under his arm. "What are you doing in New York?" he said.

"Writing a book about the longshoremen's union," the girl said. "And washing up."

He was gazing at her left cheekbone, though, and absently swatting the air.

(*"Libra ascendant. You will encounter fiery 'reminders.'*
Sign of mutable air. Easy-moving gait in 'speculation.'")

"I'm trying to find an actress I once saw who looks just like you. Can you think who it is? American. I'd have to get her past Equity."

"You could probably wangle it," she said, squinting at her letter.

"Do you know anything about unions, then?"

She gave up and said, "Are you buying plays?"

"So there, you do remember me. That's wonderful. Doesn't one roast in America." He pulled off his jacket in a hurry and left one sleeve turned inside out, like a small boy's jersey. A waiter came up and made him put it on again.

He leaned forward as if he meant to kiss her and then said in a low voice, "I'm going to give you the name of a first-rate lawyer."

"What I need is a vet for my cat," she said. "I don't think I need a lawyer."

"I can find you the best vet in New York. I know someone. But put this name down. He's the top lawyer in New York. For example, 'I can't pay you straightaway,' I had to say to him. 'That's all right,' he said. 'We can wait until doomsday, or 1973, whichever is the sooner.' 'No, you won't have to,' I told him, 'my luck's on the turn; it's going to be a tremendous year, though it's true that just now one's recovering from a few debacles.' Get out your book and write his name down. And while we're about it I'll give you the name of the best dentist in America. You'll say you shouldn't afford it here and neither should I, but in dentistry they've got the edge on us and you can't begrudge teeth. Liz says that. You've never met her. I always wanted to introduce you but there never seemed to be the chance of it. You haven't seen me since the bad time with the lawyers."

"This lawyer?"

"No, in England. My own company sued me, didn't you know? Making me carry the can. 'All right,' I said, 'sue me.' I moved out of my office the same afternoon. I found a place in West Kensington. No reason why a theatrical manager has to be in Shaftesbury Avenue and pay those rents. They tried to intimidate me by holding on to the furniture. There was a desk I was fond of, it's true. But by then I was into my new place and I felt shot of the stuff. 'All right,' I told them, 'keep it; I don't want it now, I'm perfectly happy, thanks.' That was our bad year. I didn't know it was all coming, of course, which is just as well. Fortunate that things don't happen all at the same time. Insofar as time is constituted by duration—"

He had a think, and blew his nose, noticing after a moment that her mind was fixed on his words in a way that made him feel quite light. A five-pound note that had got muddled up with his handkerchief fluttered to the floor, and he looked at it accusingly, though without making a move.

"Next month we had the burglary," he said. "Liz lost a winning I'd given her on a horse. We'd kept it in cash. You can't insure cash, as you know, but who cares, and it seemed a good present. A Christmas stocking—no, a pair of red tights, actually—filled up to here with pound notes that we'd won on a strawberry roan named Cordelia. I'd just had an idea for a way of doing *Lear* and it had brought me luck. The idea. At the time. Though the money went later, as I said. In the same swoop they took my father's silver cigarette case. The first time I ever got bashed around the earhole was when I put my dirty fingers on that cigarette case. His letters went too, for some reason." The impresario made a face. "Rotten year." But a minute later he looked buoyed up.

("You have recently had a 'bad' year. Ignore this. Gamble on 'profits.' Journeys ahead. Your assets will be enfervoured. Lucky colour gold or gilt.")

The girl rescued the five-pound note, because he was obviously going to let it lie there. "Oh, thanks very much," he said in a courtly way, stuffing it back into his handkerchief pocket. "*Lousy* year. Good riddance."

He paused, and she said to prompt him, "I heard you were poorly."

"Well, I had to have my tonsils out when we were in the middle of producing *Tamburlaine,* which meant that the stage management made a right old mess of pulling on the chariot. I daresay you heard about that joke-night among the London literati." He stared at her. If she doesn't answer me seriously, he thought, if she's listened to the chatter about me, she's had it.

"No," she said. "It came on fine the night I was there. I think it was on a truck. Have I got that right? From the prompt side."

Relieved, he talked volumes about the technical problems of chariots.

"And after the tonsils something else happened?" she said, looking for more, because he didn't seem a man to make a fuss over tonsils, but he evaded her and said only, "*Foul* year."

"What else happened?" she said, digging away.

"I couldn't seem to get back any vim, that's all. In the end I dropped in on Oliver Craddock, just out of curiosity, and he saw everything without my telling him a word."

"You mean an astrologer?"

"You're laughing at me and I laughed at myself, but he's the best astrologer in London. As I say, I wasn't feeling particularly well at that point. All right, I thought; yes, it's womanish to go to him, but they're poor times, and maybe an astrologer's a rug to put over you when you're wintering. I'm going to give you his address. I've never fancied the stars, having been a computer programmer in early life, but it may be a truth that mathematicians are often superstitious."

"I wouldn't have known you'd been in computers."

"We're not a breed."

"What made you stop?"

"It began to seem a craven sort of job. Also lonely, and without much dash, to my mind. I'd do most of it at night. I was learning at a place where we hired the computer's time and it was cheaper to get a night run. The engineer would go to sleep soon in a corner. Liz would have given me a thermos and a book. I generally didn't drop off till four or five. The computer would be burbling away and the lights would be fluttering around the console. One calls it a console and it looks much like an awful cocktail cabinet. But the nights there gave me an idea later for a psychedelic light show, so they weren't all waste. If you dozed off and the computer happened to break down, the silence generally woke you. A comforting feature of that particular model was that you could store drinks in the back of its refrigeration compartment. I'm feeling splendid, aren't you?"

A waiter came up to him and handed him an airmail copy of some newspaper. He folded it open at a page of stocks and shares, and as he was looking down the lists he gave the man two dollars.

"You tip too much, don't you?" the girl said.

"Hang on a moment. I've got to telephone," he said. She started to get up but he said, "Don't go, don't go," and hurried out of the bar, running with his body crouched and his right hand holding the newspaper low down, like a soldier carrying a slung rifle running in to the attack.

Someone came back with him to plug in a telephone. "Do you want to be on your own?" she said.

"Don't go," he said again, getting a London number and ringing his stockbroker late in the English night. She read while he talked. He has the sound of a desperado, she thought. Hanging on to the cliff face by his nails, gaining small purchase on it.

"I was just talking to my bookie," he said crisply, which was the way he treated money troubles. "While I was about it, I put a fiver for you on a nice little filly called General Motors." He had a drink, and then a double, looking at her. "You're a very pretty girl. Delicate. I don't mean unwell."

"Actually, I have seen your wife. At the Lyric one night."

"Liz has a small face, too."

No, the girl thought, it was a big, strong face, remembering it quite clearly, and then putting aside that puzzle. "What happened after the computers?"

"Liz made me stop. We wondered what to do next, because the only other thing I'd ever done was box. I was in and out of work. More out than in. I took a job at a place where they did greeting cards. We put out a lot of get-well cards and deepest sympathies, which was a bit of a con when the only thing I knew how to do apart from programming was punching people. I hadn't been any great shakes at boxing, but I'd thought as a young man that I might be. Everybody needs to shine at something, and I thought I could box. I used to have quite a complex about being beaten, but I met Liz after I'd been beaten hollow all year and she still married me."

"You looked happy, the two of you. She was wearing a red suit with red boots and a pleated shirt."

He blinked strangely.

"And you look fine now," she said, pushing on. "People revive very fast." Some people, she thought, he in her mind. The diligence of cheering up.

"Well, it's true that one isn't always sure that life can continue under its present auspices, but I am at the moment," he said, "and especially today. Oliver Craddock told me this would be a good time. 'It will be full of travel.'" He ate a peanut and went over his own words, having a perfect verbal memory, which was an aid in his profession. "'Auspicious' is something Indians often say. I had an Indian friend in the bad year, a lawyer from Udaipur who kept up my spirits when the partners were after me. 'Today is an auspicious day,' he would say. He was quite superstitious, generally leaning to one's own advantage."

And then she read, in a copy of *The Stage* that happened to be turned in her direction, a paragraph about him which made it clear that the wife whom he was talking about in the present tense had died a year ago, and that he had had a row of flops in London.

"New York's a shot in the arm," he was saying. "I've bought the biggest shows in town. I'm going to make a fortune, and your little flurry on General Motors will keep you in mink for the rest of your life. No, not mink. I can see you wouldn't like mink. Fun furs. No, I daresay they've gone already. A beautiful pale-auburn fox down to your ankles, with a high collar to turn up. You'd look like a very small Katharine Hepburn. Witty. Have you seen that thing called *Thighbone*? Do you think it'd go? Barbra Streisand wants to do it with me."

"She'd make anything go," the girl said, a second after reading a paragraph on the front page of *Variety* about two big London managements—no mention of him—that were bidding against each other for the show. "What made you want to go into the theatre?"

"Well"—and he waited to be certain he was putting it right, for she gave him scruples—"well, as we were saying, one isn't sure of the ruling hand any longer, so there is an inclination these days to take over oneself."

"Is it that? Isn't it the risk?"

"No, the control. That's what I didn't like about computers; you have to truckle. Anyway, I'm not a man of the disciplines. I thought to myself, Computers are in danger of making people furious, but the theatre as a job of work might be just the meat."

"Isn't it the gambling? The cheek?" The backbone, she thought, on her way to the newsstand.

When she got back, he was charging their drinks to himself and ordering more. "Room 605 or 505, whichever floor it is. You know it," he cried to the waiter. And "Oh, I am having a nice time!" he exclaimed to her. Another waiter came up to him then with a bundle of letters and cash that he had left behind in the foyer and forgotten. He gave him ten dollars and put the clump of valuables underneath his newspapers and a heap of message slips and theatre programs.

"Liz isn't a bit theatrical. She's Pisces, I'm Scorpio. Oliver Craddock saw it all. He said it would be hard for a time." He pulled at his tie. "When the lawsuit was beginning, before he could possibly have known about it, he wrote this down for me on a bit of paper." The impresario scribbled on a copy of *Arts-Spectacles* and turned it round to the girl.

" 'Legal, psyche-regenerative.' That's what he wrote," he said.

"What happened after the greeting cards?" she said. Some strong feeling roared along her bones.

"You could use words like 'fantastic' or 'spectacular.' I was in Cook's getting our letters because we hadn't an address at the time. We were living here and there, and I was looking for investors, so we gave a care-of-Cook's address. I was watching someone else picking up his post, a nice-looking man with a stoop, and he was reading his letters and he came to one where he cried bitterly. So I introduced myself. It was a letter describing the last hours of a friend of his. None other than the greatest mathematician in the world. You'll guess what I'm leading up to. Well, he said he was a writer, and I said I was looking for plays to invest in and why didn't he write one about his friend, and a couple of months later he'd written something pretty splendid, hadn't he? The luck began to run the other way and we made a bit of a fortune that six months. Who would think it of Cook's. Or of American Express, for that matter. A benediction from Cook's." He flapped his jacket. He had a nose like a snout, long and inquiring.

"It sounds more your doing," she said. "I don't believe much in luck."

"Ah, all I did was have an idea," he said. "Having an idea is nothing to go by."

She didn't intrude.

"Don't you be nice to me. I'm known as a bit of a bastard," he said proudly, heaving the pile of newspapers onto the floor and in the process dropping his wallet out of his jacket pocket. "Don't you be taken in, I'm not to be trusted," he said, noticing that his spectacles were steamed up. He rubbed them with a paper napkin and then put them away in his jacket because they seemed ugly in front of this pretty girl. As he was doing that, he saw the paragraph about himself in *The Stage* and planted his shoe over it. " 'Things will improve from May 25th' " he repeated to himself silently, but moving his lips a little, which the girl noticed. He looked at her and said, adopting roguishness, "Would you like to come on a long journey with me? While I do a deal? Neptune is moving into Scorpio. I've got two first-class tickets. One always has two. On the firm."

But he's the firm, she thought.

"The most splendid hotel in America," he said. "The modern Chartres."

(*"Things will improve from May 25th. Forget bad 'symptoms.'"*)

"When?" she said.

"I'm going tonight," he said, scuffing the paragraph in *The Stage* hard with his foot as if he were rubbing cigarette ash into the carpet. "I won't promise to keep my hands off you, mind. And I'll be busy. It's a business trip. You won't see much of me." Then he said seriously, "It's a stingy offer."

People may blunder, she thought, and their actions can still have a fine echo; or they may act all right and the echo can be bad. "What plane?" she said. She paid for her own ticket, as it turned out. He forgot.

On the plane, which had armrests a foot wide, made in a plastic that looked like jellied gold lamé, he pretended suddenly to have remembered something and drew a rumpled piece of paper out of his wallet.

"Oliver Craddock wrote this down for me the first time I saw him and I'd forgotten all about it," he said. He smoothed the paper with his fingers and gave it to her. "I haven't looked at it since," he said, but it was much handled. She gave it back after reading it, and he went through it carefully as though he had never seen it. "Oliver Craddock said last year, 'There will be a removal of something or someone around May 25th.' Liz said, 'Christ, I hope it doesn't mean we're going to have to move.' 'No,' I said. 'We'll stay put in old West Ken,' but Oliver had seen it all, and I came to America the first time on May

25th. You may say an aeroplane isn't much, but it's a sign of activity."

(*"Do nothing 'more' in the present year. Neptune is moving into Sagittarius. Spark your income. You are very 'tired,' but this will change."*)

"Isn't it splendiferous?" he said in the hotel, gazing up. The lobby soared: twenty-eight floors high. At the top a glass cocktail bar slowly revolved, and drinkers exclaimed gaily at the changing spectacle of industrial buildings under construction. The racket of cement mixing was masked by the sound of Muzak. Lifts of glass and gilded plastic in the shape of water beetles darted up and down the outside of concrete columns four hundred feet high. Greenery dripped like candle wax into the lobby from the surrounding balconies; possibly *was* wax. Water lilies in a pool outside the coffee area were made of tin sprayed to look like copper. The impresario and the girl stood and watched, both shy. The hostess of the coffee place thought they were waiting for a table and corrected them for not standing in the queue. She was wearing a red velvet skirt cut like a skating skirt, with an alderman's neck chain slung round her hips and clanking between her legs. A diamanté brooch on her chest read "Miss Christmas." "No room," she said.

The impresario got two bedrooms. "In case Liz rings," he said to the girl, handing her a separate key and holding the back of her neck. She nodded, wondering why on earth, since Liz was dead and they were obviously going to be sharing a room. They had a drink and went to bed, and afterward he talked to her about deals and projects.

"You like America, don't you?" she said, raising her voice

because of the uproar of building outside the hotel and the din of business conventions inside it.

"I went to Los Angeles on the last trip, and Las Vegas," he said. "Let's have another bottle of champagne. Las Vegas is a beautiful place. Perks one up. You perk me up. You've got to go there."

"I've been there," she said, but he rode over that, bent on ignoring his unreasonable jealousy that she had gone with anyone else.

"I was feeling a bit tired," he said, "but it was wonderful there. I took Liz. Huge carpeted slopes in the hotel, like a golf course."

He turned away to the bedside table and found a souvenir sack of nickels from Las Vegas among the things he had unpacked from his pockets. "Here," he said, and threw it to her. "Save it for when I take *you* gambling in Las Vegas," juggling this chance in his head with the unthinkable odds that he would never see her again. "And then I went to Los Angeles, and I spent Thanksgiving on Malibu Beach, and there was a picture window"—he stared around him at the shoebox room and rejected it—"let's not exaggerate, but it would stretch from here to the lift. You should have seen the bed. It would have taken seven. It was as wide as a bus. What a beautiful day, right at the end of November. I went swimming, and I was so happy I cried into the sea for three-quarters of an hour. I don't know why. I never do that. Then I saw Rock Hudson and closed a deal. Well, and then I went on to Rome to look at a Goldoni production and I had to see the Pope, but I tell you —I hope you're not Catholic—the sight of the old pullet being cheered up the aisle of St. Peter's . . . They don't know how to deal with the times. Children living in the streets, peasants arriving from Sicily without an idea . . . Anyway, I signed all the talent in Rome."

The Muzak played "Raindrops Keep Fallin' on My Head" and they talked about Italy and then about nothing very much. Her chin was like the heel of a child's foot. "I signed a beautiful new actress," he said, leaning on his elbow and gazing at the girl. "Bilingual. Wonderful wrists. Green eyes, which is unusual. And the bone structure!" He stroked the girl's collarbone devotedly. "I'm going to groom her, and then I'm going to show her to the National Theatre. She's the Latin Maggie Smith. I want to put her with Larry and John G. and Ralph on Broadway and see the chemistry."

He gave her some more champagne and she asked if he had children.

"Three sons," he said. "Fourteen, sixteen, and twenty-one. Our greatest joy is that the twenty-one-year-old wants to go into the car industry."

Our.

"He's got the mathematical background that's needed for the future," the impresario said.

"You don't want him to go into the theatre with you? Or be your bookie in the City?"

"The flair for getting away with things doesn't descend unto the second generation."

Then he went to his own room. "I've got to lay a few more bets," he said.

A couple of hours later he rang to ask her to pick him up. The Muzak reached a gap as she was about to knock on the door and she could hear he was being told by the hotel that his credit wasn't good. "There must be some mistake," he was saying with an air. "The computers as usual, I suppose, but you'd better ring my solicitors and ask them to cable you the cash. I'll give you the number later. I've got an international call coming through."

She drew away to the balcony over the lobby, feeling incapable, looking down at the bawling men in dinner jackets far below and the women with stiff hair. After a while she went back again, and heard him talking to his broker about checks that were bouncing.

She asked him to come to her room so as not to overhear any more, and then they went downstairs in an express lift: a glass-and-gilt beetle that hurtled the twenty-eight floors in nine and a half seconds. He hung on to the semicircular rail around the outer edge, where they were standing because the businessmen who had got in after them had jostled them there, and she saw that his eyes were closed and that he had gone gray with fear about the drop. "I love you," she whispered under the Muzak. His eyelids fluttered for a second and stayed shut until they reached the ground floor.

They went out, he in a white suit, and he told her they were going to shoot pool. He clutched her shoulders on the way: a big shambles of a man, with shapely legs and a tendency to put on his overcoat with the collar turned inward. "Pool always perks me up," he said. "We'll have some more champagne in a moment. Champagne's the best drink. It doesn't give you a hangover if you remember to get down half a pint of water before you go to sleep. It's not easy to lay your hands on decent champagne here, but I know the manager."

"I can't believe my good luck sometimes," he said to her later in bed. "You're always in such demand."

Then he paused, and sounded tired, and said, "I've got something I must advise you about. If you are to prosper, as you should—" and she waited, but he had dropped into sleep like a stone.

He woke in a fury two hours afterward, and said that she had upset his rhythm and that he had to make some calls. From his room, not this, he seemed to mean. "I'll come with you," she said, risking intrusiveness. They dressed quickly and he again closed his eyes in terror while they were riding in the lift. His white suit by this time was crumpled and the Muzak seemed louder than ever. "I love you," she whispered under the din of other people's exclamations about the phenomenal machine.

They went into his room. "I'll give you a drink and then you'd better leave," he said angrily, clutching the back of her neck with great fondness, as before. "I want to ring Liz."

She went down to the lobby to settle the bill so far for both their rooms, and then changed her mind and paid only for her own and the booze. While she was waiting for the computer to do whatever it had to do, she rested her elbows on the counter with her back to it and the man next to her said in a heavy voice, "Are you an actress?"

"No, I'm just here with somebody."

"Come have a drink with me. You're a very lovely girl. You're not a feminist, are you?"

"I can't. Thanks."

"You *are* a feminist."

He went on needling her. "Are you an intellectual?"

"No, I do washing up."

"You're putting me on. Why would a lovely girl like you do dishwashing?"

"I need the loot."

"*Any* guy would keep you! You *are* an intellectual! What are you trying to *do* to me!"

She had to wait until her passport came back because she had cashed a traveller's check to pay the bill. She watched the lobby and suddenly saw that, in one of the lifts hurling down the middle of this Chartres, the impresario was standing with his hands clutching the railing. It didn't seem that he was looking for her, since he immediately went up again. Merely testing a hallucination, perhaps. Or himself.

She knocked loudly at the door of his room and carried in a tray of caviar. He was on the telephone.

"Marlon, it's a wonderful play for you, and Sophia wants to do it with us. Let me know tomorrow morning, eh?" he said.

Then he had some caviar and rang Italy and said, "Sophia, this play I sent that Marlon's going to do, he only wants to do it with you. Ring tomorrow, eh?"

Then he rang some film company in London and asked for one of the most junior men in the public-relations office, and the girl could hear the phone being put down on him.

"Is this your caviar or mine?" said the impresario. "I ordered you some. I wish Liz were here. What are you thinking?"

"Nothing."

"When people say it that fast, it always means they were thinking about something in particular."

"Nothing."

"I've got a lot to do. I've got to get some sleep," the impresario said, eating a spoonful of caviar and looking at a column about grosses in *Variety*. "Marlon and Sophia," he said. "Quite a double. '*Molto* boffo.' What do you think of ringing Albie Finney? I could get Albie. He's a friend of mine."

She went to sit beside him on the bed and read something tinny and long-winded about the recovery of Wall Street. "Have you got a lot riding on the market's getting better?" she said.

"A fair amount."

"Is it what you live off? More than the theatre?"

He stayed silent, quite obstinately, and she switched tone and said, "This is a trip about cheering up, isn't it? About keeping one's spirits up if one's a late capitalist?"

She was grinning as she said it, but he didn't take that in and yelled at her about Women's Lib claptrap. After a bit, he took off his debonair jacket and lay back on the bed in a beautiful fluted shirt, much creased, holding her newspaper over his head to look at the article she had been reading. She stabbed a finger at a line she remembered laughing about.

"What is it?" he said, declining to be humored.

" 'Investors used the summer doldrums as an excuse to stay away from the market in droves,' " she read out. "The shirkers."

"Ho hum," he said.

A couple of hours later, when he had been talking non-stop on the telephone, she was sitting in a chair half asleep.

"I'm going to make a fortune," he said. "Oliver Craddock was right. What *were* you thinking when you wouldn't tell me?"

"Nothing. Sorry, I've gummed up. It wasn't anything."

He threw a piece of ice at her and called her frigid.

She said in a rage that she had been thinking it was rough on him to belong to a society with a theology of gambling.

"You're in it too, mate," he said.

"Not half as much as Oliver Craddock."

"Marxist garbage."

She flounced into the bathroom, and then tried to think how to flounce out again in any way that would get her past his indispensable face and into the bloody lift. The telephone went, which was a possible cue, and she came out and heard somebody's secretary giving him a brushoff. He let only a moment go by before filling a teaspoon full of caviar and feeding it to her.

(*"Don't give way to 'anxieties.' Hearty awakening is in you."*)

"What time is it in London?" he said.

She looked at the fob watch round her neck. "Eight in the morning. Don't you ever stop working?"

"Do you keep that watch on London time when you're away?"

"Yes."

"Who do you miss, then?"

"England."

He set the hotel alarm clock, touched. "There's an hour before anyone'll thank me for ringing them back," he said defiantly. And then he wondered who she was in love with in London, to have kept a watch on another time; and asked himself why in Christ she had come with him, in that case; and at the same moment reflected about some plays, for he truly liked the theatre.

"Need for subplots," he muttered when she thought he was asleep. "No, for sub-characters, to say there's something else. Fortinbras coming in at the end, when Hamlet's dead and everyone's dead. They're always cutting Fortinbras. I tell you, I wouldn't care to put on *Hamlet* without Fortinbras."

"Who were you with at the Lyric? Who was it in the red suit? What are we pretending about?"

"Red suit?"

"It wasn't Liz, was it?"

"No. Liz died a long while ago."

"Why didn't you tell me that before?"

He went silent, so she apologized.

"It was ages ago," he said roughly. "I'm not where they think I am. This is a *good* year."

She got up and stomped around.

The other room would be for telephone calls about being broke, of course.

"Come to *bed*," he said. "I've got a lot of deals in a minute."

She wished there were the faintest chance that he would drop being breezy. She lay down, and he drifted off, and five minutes later the central heating was hissing and clanging like a forge. He raised his head. "It's all right," she whispered under the noise, and he settled down again on his side with his back to her. Pause. Asleep, apparently.

"The truth is," he said, "I've been very eager to see you. They think I'm a dead duck, but it's not been a time you could write off. If I sleep through the alarm, will you wake me? Scorpio is coming into Aquarius. I've got to talk to my bookie."

After a pause he said, "Go if you want to."

It happened that she was propped on her elbow and could see that he had his fingers crossed.

"Thanks a million, but no thanks," she said, and he uncrossed them.

"Will you live with me?" she said, after thinking about it.

"Of course. Why the hell didn't you ask me before?" he said, and went to sleep at once. A few minutes later he was jerking around in the grip of an atrocious dream, and she woke him up.

"Go away. I'm asleep," he said.

"Weren't you having a bad dream?"

"No, just strenuous."

Nobody's Business

➤➤➤-➤➤➤-➤➤➤ A big man with a municipal face was swimming toward Edward and Emily Prendergast across the glassy Mediterranean.

"Morning!" he shouted to Sir Edward, who is a judge. A tall, skinny man, with a soft voice that sometimes strikes the court as coming from behind his left ear. He has been married to Emily for nearly forty years. Emily is a woman of obscure stylishness who gardens, carpenters, reads science fiction, bottles fruit and pickles according to Elizabethan family recipes, and writes the most popular low comedies of the century. They are done weekly on the radio in the lunch hour, and people listen to them in factories by the million.

The big man splashed up to Edward and held his hand out of the water cordially, bobbing up and down.

"How do you do?" Edward said, turning his august profile with a politeness that Emily didn't believe necessarily to be lasting.

"Long time no see," said the big man.

"Have we met?" said Edward.

There he goes, Emily thought gaily.

"In the B.B.C. canteen," the big man said. "You came to pick up your lady wife one day after a rehearsal. You won't remember. Long ago. I was the producer."

Two striking bodies were swimming after the big man, lifting themselves rhythmically out of the water with the butterfly stroke. Magnificent tanned shoulders consecutively emerged. One pair male, one female, probably, Emily thought.

"I don't believe you know Maximilian Keller," the big man said, making introduction gestures awkwardly a few inches above the surface of the sea, "and Jo-Ann Sills. Maximilian is from the University of Basel and Jo-Ann is from the University of California at Los Angeles."

"I'm the archivist who bothered you last April, and I wondered if you'd had any second thoughts," Jo-Ann said to Edward. Her long hair spread out in the water around her.

"Second thoughts about what?" said Edward.

"About letting us have your papers for the Sir Edward Prendergast Collection and the Lady Prendergast Collection— the *Emily Firle* Collection."

"The only papers we seem to keep are bills, and they're for the accountant," Emily said.

"But you must have kept your manuscripts," the beautiful girl said, and turned her head to Edward in the sea. "Your office surely must have kept your briefs over the years."

Emily stayed quiet, treading water and wondering where the others' breath for talking came from.

"And what about your memorabilia?" said Jo-Ann.

"*Is* there an Edward Prendergast Collection?" said Edward. "*What* Lady Prendergast Collection? What the hell are memorabilia?"

" 'Emily Firle,' I said," Jo-Ann answered in a voice of quartz.

"Don't ignore Women's Liberation," Emily said privately to Edward.

He made one of his expostulatory noises, seldom employed but powerful, and looked at her carefully from ten feet away in the water, lifting his spectacles to the bridge of his nose and then having to peer under them because they were crusted with salt, raising his head rather merrily, like a sea lion balancing a ball on its snout. "Are you all right?" he said, moving round so that he had his back to the others.

"Bored," she said softly.

"What's the big man's name?" he said in his lowest voice.

"I don't know." It was someone she had been to bed with. Long ago. Nothing. But indecent to forget. She made an effort: "David Willoughby, I think."

"Maximilian and Jo-Ann wrote a joint thesis about you both," Willoughby said loudly.

Emily had turned onto her back to save her strength and was staring at the sun.

"About us?" she said, turning upright again to go on treading water.

The talk in the sea lasted for another half an hour. Maximilian said grimly that his special interest was humor, and Jo-Ann said that her topic in the thesis had been the theme of male chauvinism in Edward's published legal opinions.

"What do you think of Women's Lib?" she said to Emily.

"I should think it's quite right, probably. Is anyone else tired?"

" 'Probably'? I hear doubt here," Maximilian said, raising a finger astutely out of the water.

"Shall we go in?" Emily said.

"Doubt, when you're generally so decided? Crisp? In your dialogue?" Maximilian said with disappointment.

"Doubt is the courtesy of the intellect," Edward said, sounding irritable and throwing his voice like a cat.

"And that seems to me a very uncharacteristic thing for *you* to say," Willoughby said firmly. He lifted his hand out of the water to smooth his hair. Emily tried to remember if she had ever known in the days of seeing him that he was such a strong swimmer, but nothing much came back.

At the same time she said, exhausted, "Not really uncharacteristic. If it weren't that a judge has to decide a case, quite a few of Edward's legal opinions would probably end in a question mark."

Maximilian drew out a plastic notebook from underwater with his left hand and started to make a note in it with his right, using a gadget pencil with his name on it in gold.

Emily only then took in that the others were not swimming at all but standing on the bottom, and that the reason she was worn out from treading water was that she was a good eight or twelve inches shorter than the rest. It made her laugh, and she sank. She had not had a violent case of laughing for years. She came up once and tried to get out a cry for help to the others standing there, but the laughing gripped her lungs and they thought she was fooling. She choked and spat out some seawater and then swallowed a lungful as she went into a spasm again. She sank slowly to the bottom and opened her eyes and saw the legs of the four underwater. One pair Californian legs, one pair Swiss legs, one pair forgotten legs, one pair Edward's legs. My finishing-school clothes list: One pair plimsolls, one pair best silk stockings, one Liberty bodice, amen, we give Thee most humble and hearty thanks, we Thine unworthy servants. Damn. I can remember everything. Life up to its old clichés again. I suppose it means I'm drowning. The three of them are presiding over us like a tribunal. She lost track.

Her husband, seventy-four, was the one who fished her out. Willoughby helped. The hale and hearty young archivists stood by, worried that she might die—worried partly because of the venerable old man's fever that she shouldn't, and partly because of professional affront at the possibility of all that memorabilia going west.

"You have an immense output," Willoughby said severely to Emily a few weeks later, leaning over her desk as if he were a judge himself. "Would you say that you were first rate or second rate?"

She and Edward were sitting together in their Dorset drawing room, in their chairs on each side of the fireplace, where they always sat. Jo-Ann and Maximilian and Willoughby were across the room, where visitors always sat. A stenographer was taking things down. The archivists had won.

"You don't need to answer the question," Edward said to her.

"A bit ropy," she said to Willoughby.

"The arranging of work in a hierarchy is a fat-headed process," Edward said to Willoughby.

"Would you deny that Lady Prendergast's work has literary worth, then? Just because it's humorous?" Willoughby said to Edward.

"Just because she's produced over a thousand scripts and books?" Maximilian said. "Personally, I rank the *œuvre* very high."

Œuvre, Emily thought. Blimey.

"So do I," Edward said. "But then, for me, *she* ranks high, don't you see."

"But how would you place your work, though?" Maximilian said to Emily. "In the event of your death, will it stand up?"

"I shouldn't think so, should you?" she said.

"Gas about posterity," Edward said, making a sort of barking noise and then lighting his pipe.

"Huh?" said Willoughby.

"What matters is the needs which art answers," Edward said. "I think that may be right. Could we have crumpets for tea?"

" 'I think that may be right,' " Emily said. "I like the way you say that."

Willoughby was shaking his head at the stenographer. "You can leave all that out. Everything after 'which art answers.' It wouldn't signify. Don't bother about taking anything down when you see me shaking my head."

"Conversations about lousiness," Emily said to Edward.

"Yes," Edward said. They ran over a few in their minds, having acquired the same references.

"Huh?" said Maximilian.

"She means there can be a certain quality to the rotten," Edward said.

"Can we go into that?" said Maximilian, and Willoughby signalled to the stenographer to start again.

"No," Edward said.

After a pause, Emily said, "There was once a very popular act called the Apple Blossom Sisters. They were popular because they were so lousy. They were singers and they couldn't sing a note in tune. The management would put up a screen in front of them and provide the audience with bad eggs and moldy tomatoes to pelt them with."

"You're not suggesting you're one of the Apple Blossom Sisters?" Maximilian said.

"Probably," Edward said. "She has a low opinion of herself."

"Then how does she go on? Producing this pretty remarkable work?"

"She doesn't always. There are halts. Quite long, for her. In that case, she will carpenter or go on a dig. An archeological dig. You know that she read archeology by correspondence when she was at finishing school. And then she will take a few days off from seeing anybody except me and do a bit of work. I've never been made much aware of it. She does it at that desk and I'll think she's writing letters."

"She works easily, then," Maximilian said. "In your very different and distinguished field, do you?"

Edward barked again through his nose.

Emily said, "Of course he does. But he stomps off to have a think now and then. There's always the possibility of making a terminal ass of yourself, isn't there?"

"Is that a mule?" said Maximilian, in his perfect English, making a note. "The terminal ass? Is that a demotic idiom?"

"Could we talk now about humor?" said Maximilian.

"Couldn't we have the crumpets?" said Edward.

"What about having a kipper as well? What about having a kipper to our tea?" said Emily.

"What an interesting preposition," Maximilian said, writing it down.

"Our friends have an idea for a joint lecture on educational television about the mechanics of humor," Willoughby said. "To study it as though it were a problem of engineering. Which it is, of course, as you of all people know."

"With your ear. With your technical sense," Maximilian said.

"Can you and Jo-Ann deal with a kipper?" Emily said. "They're rather full of bones in England. We don't debone them here, I'm afraid."

"The idea is," said Maximilian, motioning Jo-Ann to stand up, "to show a television audience the effect of trousers falling down." He started to unstrap his belt and then let his trousers fall to the floor. "One would show them falling at the usual speed and hear the laughs." He pulled them up and fastened the belt again with a scholarly expression. "Then one would show what happened if the speed were different." He waved to Jo-Ann to stand behind his back. "One would see them lowered very slowly." The pretty girl behind him let down his trousers inch by inch. "Don't rush it," he said. The trousers reached his ankles. He looked up and said majestically, "You see, it isn't funny."

"Actually, I thought it was almost funnier that time," Edward said, freezing his face, as he was used to having to do in court.

Maximilian saw nothing and said, "It would be interesting to observe whether one got the same effect by slowing up the, say, motion of a shoe on a banana skin."

"Born?" said Jo-Ann to Emily.

"Edward was born in London and I was born in Russia. Why does one go so much by where people are born, I wonder. Where were you born?"

"Rumania," Jo-Ann said.

"There, you see, and yet you seem completely Californian to me. Do you feel Californian?"

"Do you mind not answering our questions with so many questions, Lady Prendergast?" Maximilian said.

"I'm sorry," Emily said.

"And how did you leave Russia?"

"I lived with my uncle. I was an orphan. My grandparents got married in an old people's home. It was rather a jolly occasion."

"That doesn't answer the question. How did you leave?"

"It's not very interesting. I had English relations. What I remember, as I say, is my grandparents' getting married in Russia. They'd been living together for many years. When they grew poor they had to be shut away in an old people's home, because poverty didn't officially exist in the new state. It doesn't officially exist in America either, would you say? So they had to disappear. They had a fine wedding. They were aged eighty-nine and ninety. Everyone was in black because their best clothes were for funerals, and everyone danced. There was only one record, and that was the Slovene national anthem. Somebody had brought it with him. It wasn't quite the thing, but it was very beautiful."

"And then?"

"She came to England," Edward said. "Her father was a playwright. He died soon after she was born."

"Yes, we know that," said Maximilian. "It's in *Who's Who*."

"What I was going to tell you is that he had written her a part in one of his plays. A non-speaking part. It was her inheritance, so to say. May I have a glass of water until you've decided about the kippers? He thought she could always be an actress in a pinch, you see. He wrote the part so that she could always support herself in exile if she didn't speak the language."

"Edward and I met in England in 1920," Emily said. "I'd been kicked by a horse and lost two front teeth and he took me out to lunch and gave me asparagus. Asparagus is extremely difficult to eat without front teeth, because it means pulling the things through the side molars and it makes a mess of the lipstick. Those were the days when girls wore lipstick."

"You still do," Edward said. "I like it better."

"It was a very fine lunch, to my mind."

"And do you care for the times?" said Willoughby to Edward.

"Inadequate," said Edward.

"Without belief? Without intellectual system?"

"No, thin news coverage. We both prefer the Washington *Post*. We get it by airmail."

"Mr. Willoughby means the age, I think," Emily said. "Well, as we're in the presence of two students—postgraduate students—I daresay you'll take me to be sucking up, but the times are rather interesting, don't you find? The music and the clothes and the courage and so on. The nerve. Something here, don't you think? One doesn't want to go."

"Go? What did you say that for?" Edward said.

Maximilian laughed as if someone had made a joke.

"No question of it," she said to Edward. "I'm not a quitter."

"No," he said. "You hung on for twelve years."

"Isn't it odd, sitting here without quite having the face to touch each other? It's like the time when you were in hospital. When we could talk on the telephone every day and I couldn't come to see you."

"Why not?" said Jo-Ann.

"Because he was married to someone else then."

"Male chauvinist. Why did you put up with it?" Jo-Ann said to Emily. "Letting the man have it both ways at once. They always do."

"Well, it was a poor time, but it improved rapidly."

"Where were you born?" said Jo-Ann.

"We've asked that already. Russia. Don't you remember?" Willoughby said.

"I used to have a memory, like, but my mind has blown," Jo-Ann said.

"My dear girl," Emily said, worried.

"I got into this tragical area of experience, but I feel as if I'm coming out of it now," said Jo-Ann.

"What friend's voice were you speaking in just then? Are you going to a therapist?"

"Yes."

"Well, never mind," Emily said.

"Of course, my wife *holds* with the world," Edward said to Willoughby.

"You don't?" said Willoughby.

"Not necessarily."

"Is he a demonstrative man?" Willoughby said to Emily, pointing at Edward with his pen.

"No," said Edward.

"Yes," said Emily.

"What was that about hospital?" Maximilian asked.

"Edward could tell you."

"They put me in the bin because I suddenly had a talking jag," Edward said. "I couldn't stop chatting. I talked non-stop one day for twenty-three hours. Even with Emily I didn't shut up, and we have always had the capacity for shutting up. The doctors told me I shouldn't talk so much. I said, 'I know that as well as you; the fact I can't do anything about it is my complaint, don't you see. Cure me of that and I'll be well.'"

Emily said to Willoughby, "You must tell the stenographer to stop, and we'll have tea."

"Not till we're finished," Willoughby said with an edge in his voice, looking at Emily. "And then what, pray? Was it when we knew each other?"

"Did you know each other well?" said Edward.

"Very well," said Willoughby.

"I'm sorry. Is that troubling?" Emily said to Edward.

"No," he said, looking as if it were.

"The hospitalization was when you and Mr. Willoughby knew each other?" said Maximilian, motioning the stenographer to attend.

"Yes," Emily said. "He was having a small breakdown. Edward was."

"You betrayed him when he was having a breakdown?" Willoughby said. "And you didn't tell me?"

"There was no reason that I could think of to tell you, and some reason not to."

"You betrayed him when he was having a breakdown?" Willoughby said again censoriously, his face looming over the desk.

"It seemed at the time that he might not have much need of intimacy. By temperament, not have much need of intimacy."

"And?"

"I had. Is it very hot?"

"Yes," Edward said. He loosened his tie.

"That's the tie I like," she said, opening one of their two copies of the Washington *Post* and burying herself behind it.

He looked at her sandals. "She's not very forthcoming always about what's going on at the back of her mind," he said after a time in a soft voice to Jo-Ann, "but I can generally tell something about it from the way she moves her toes. She wears sandals a good deal, and bare feet. We were on holiday in the Aegean when I was getting better from this talking thing and she was reading *Crime and Punishment*, and I used to watch her toes and wonder which part she had got to. I could make a fair guess."

He leaned over Emily's shoulder to see what she was reading and turned back to his own copy of the paper. "Where's that part in mine?" he said jealously, rattling the pages.

"Middle column of page nine," she said.

He found it and grew absorbed.

"How worried were you, in those days, about him? When I knew you?" said Willoughby.

"Oh dear. You think I did it to take my mind off," Emily said. "Well, perhaps I did. He was very distant then."

"Harsh," Willoughby said.

"No, distant," Edward said. "Though the effect for her was probably harsh." He put out his hand in her direction and then used the movement to tap the ash from his pipe.

"You see, he's very interested in making distinctions," Emily said. "It's the legal mind."

"I also used to have a temper," Edward said, "but it seems to be drawn off now in work."

Emily came in with a tray of tea.

"Edward made this tray when he was doing handcrafts in the bin," she said. "You can see that he didn't give himself the time to finish it. He made a quick getaway. He was having quite a bad nervous breakdown, as it turned out—"

"You said a small breakdown," Maximilian said.

"—but when he heard what the fees would be if he stayed he decided that he was hanged if he was going to spend all that money on being upset. So he drove himself away again. He had committed himself, you see, so he was technically free to go, but they apparently lock the gates on patients all the same." She poured tea. "It meant breaking the gates down. He did it with the back bumper of the car. Do you want some sponge fingers? The Daimler was barely dented."

"Why did you stay together?" Jo-Ann said.

"You don't have to answer the question," Edward said again.

"*Stare decisis,*" Emily said after a pause.

"What?" said Jo-Ann.

"It's the principle behind precedent," Edward said, looking at her. "The principle in the law. It means 'to stand by decided matters.'"

Jo-Ann said scornfully, "Instead of hanging loose."

Maximilian said, "Instead of deciding a case fresh. On its merits. The law is in love with the past."

"The law is an ass," said Willoughby.

"It's foolish not to draw on the past," Emily said. "People shouldn't have to start from the beginning every time."

"Why not? I was unhappily married once," Jo-Ann said, "and I decided the hell with it, I can't go *on* with this. My ex-husband and I just weren't meshing. It took me forever to find the maturity to say to myself how bad it was."

"But how old are you, then?" said Emily.

"Twenty-two. He had impotency fears and I was having trouble in analysis. He had a wonderful brain, but I guess we didn't know how to make it in bed. We tried to work it out. I went to a sensitivity-training center and I learned body language, but it didn't help my marriage, because I was a tool of male imperialism and that was what I was really resenting all the time. So then I freed myself and had my first lesbian relationship and now I live on my own." She looked lonely.

"What's body language?" said Edward.

"Well, like, the way you're sitting now—it tells me you're interested in me. It's a giving position."

"What about my wife?"

"She's interested in me, too. That's a giving position, too." Jo-Ann looked around the room. "David's in a hostile position. I guess he's feeling excluded. I guess you two have a lot going for you. You're both hot right now and you've been hot all your lives."

"What?" said Edward.

"Not 'what,' 'hot,'" Maximilian said.

"I know that. I said 'What?' " said Edward, lowering his voice dangerously again.

" 'Hot' means in demand," Willoughby said.

"Good lord," Emily said, turning to Maximilian. "Like the hot side of a record. Well, how very kind of you. But even if it were true it wouldn't be the sort of fact to interest one in a person, would it?"

"Then how would you explain the relationship, leaving sexuality aside?" Maximilian said. "That's one of the things we've got to explore."

"Why leave sexuality aside, pray?" Edward said. Then he took a pause and Emily looked at him, and he looked at her. After a while he turned back to Jo-Ann. "For some people," he said, "sexuality is the water they swim in. Though I can see that for others it's toy ducks in the bath."

This man has always been a great study, Emily thought.

Maximilian, wanting to make sure he had got things right, repeated in German to Willoughby what Edward had just said, and Willoughby, who spoke German, nodded wanly. It was not a particularly comforting conversation for him to hear. Emily noticed that and gave him and herself a sherry.

"It's sometimes extremely difficult to be translated," she said talkatively to the three catechizers. "Do you know, Freud's 'Beyond the Pleasure Principle' becomes in Japanese 'Happiness Lying on the Other Side of the Water.' " She paused. "Though perhaps that's what he meant, of course, and maybe the English is wrong, too. What is it in German?"

"I'll look it up," Maximilian said, making a note. "Do you write first drafts in Russian?"

"No," Emily said, "and I don't do drafts much. I just bash it out. In English."

"So Sir Edward forced his language on you," Jo-Ann said.

"No, I had an English governess. And I like English, you see. My stuff seems to get into an awful pickle when it's translated."

"That's because you've always been in the mainstream of the English popular tradition," said Maximilian.

"It didn't feel very popular to me. The first things I did came a cropper. Has anyone pinched my spectacle case? Well, they weren't up to much, I don't suppose. A great man in those days who was trying to be encouraging told me I had a terrific eye for English weather. A great critic. It took me months to get over it."

"You regret the Edwardian summers?" said Maximilian.

"Lowering of you to expect me to remember. Though I suppose one looks quite old."

"We *are* old," said Edward.

"Some of the summers in the twenties and the thirties were glorious. And there were those evil beauties during the Battle of Britain. But then again, they've been very fine lately, haven't they?"

"Anything you'd like to have been able to keep about the past?" Maximilian asked.

"Not except from a technical point of view. And there was a time when one functioned better, of course."

"Technical?"

"It's a pity about godmothers and spinster aunts. They always had an interesting part to play in my sort of stuff. It's the same with mothers-in-law. One rather misses their ferocity in the work of the moment. You find you can't get the same effect with, say, shop assistants." She paused. "There may be hope in secretaries."

"There's a mouse behind the wainscot," Edward said.

Maximilian told the stenographer not to bother until he raised his hand.

"I'm afraid it might even be a rat," Emily said.

Edward listened and said, "Too scrabbly for a rat."

" 'Life's mouse-like flitting,' " said Willoughby.

"Who wrote that?" Emily said, turning toward him and leaning over the arm of the chair. "I meant to ask you a long time ago and I forgot to. I remember your saying it a long time ago."

"Pushkin," said Willoughby.

"You'd better get the exterminator in, Emily," Edward said, again in his lowered voice, which was a habit famous in court at points when an inexperienced barrister hadn't known where to stop.

"He came today," Emily said. "Pempie and he got on."

"Who's Pempie?" said Maximilian, still signally uninterested in all this as material.

"Our secretary," Emily said. "He wanted to take her out. I believe she's rather at a loose end, but she said she couldn't seem to fancy an exterminator.

"But on the other hand," Emily went on after a wait, "the girl also said to me suddenly one day, when I thought she was trying to read back dictation, 'I can't get through the spring without a man.' We were in the middle of working out a plot. It struck me about her, you know."

"Your plots are cast iron," Maximilian said.

"Well, they haven't the structure of a lawyer's work," she said. "I'm all right as long as I know where things are going, but it's not on a par with planning a legal argument."

"You betrayed him when he was having a breakdown?" Willoughby said again. "Suppose *I'd* been having the breakdown. Would you have betrayed me?"

Emily said over him, "—as long as one knows where things are going, don't you find?" And then, with as much of an answer to his question as she felt like mustering, "I've tried to explain. Couldn't we talk about home perms or cucumber sandwiches?"

"You haven't answered his question," Maximilian said. "Do you mind if I tell you what I really think?"

"Not especially," Emily said with a pause. "After all, it's what life does all the time, isn't it? Though I rather wish *people* wouldn't do it. One doesn't resent it so much when life does. This really is a bit like the Inquisition. The three of you sitting there. There's something I keep trying to remember about you. Well, anyway, don't let's get occult. I don't like occultism, do you? That reminds me. Pempie is terrifically keen on auspicious signs, and she cheered up no end the day after the exterminator, because she drew a winning ticket in the village raffle. Everyone around had donated whatever prize he could. The butcher gave a turkey, and the hairdresser gave a shampoo and set, and a rather humorless psychiatrist who commutes to Portsmouth gave an hour's consultation. Pempie wanted to go to the psychiatrist because she's very keen on astrology and sends away for readings. I believe she associates psychiatry with palmistry. But in the end something prevailed and she had the shampoo and set. I'll get some ice, shall I?"

"I don't know how you dare," Edward said to Willoughby while she was out of the room. "Bring up the breakdown I had all those years ago. That time. When you know perfectly well that it—"

"—painful?" said Maximilian.

"—that she's got amnesia about the time when she nearly drowned," Edward said. His temper rose, and his voice fell. "I don't know how you dare. She troubles a good deal about the three hours that she's lost. She wants them back. People want their lives back."

"Were you against capital punishment in this country?" Maximilian said.

"I gave you the press cuttings about that," said Willoughby, without much grace. "He's on record, along with all the other straight-liberal-plank reformers."

"Some ass of a doctor told her that her laughing was a sign that she was trying to kill herself," Edward said.

"Perhaps she was," said Willoughby.

Edward said, "You don't know her very well. It was a sign that she thought something was funny."

"Who can tell?" said Willoughby. "Perhaps it was a sign that she'd only just realized she'd done something wrong with her life."

"Doesn't everyone?" Maximilian said, and Edward looked at him with interest and regard for the first time.

"While she's out of the room," Jo-Ann said, "tell us why the marriage has lasted. When you intimidate her so much."

"*What?*" said Edward.

"Exploit her," Jo-Ann said, and Edward's look blocked her. "All right, then," she said, "tell us anything you admire about her."

"I love her."

"Anything you *admire* about her. Apart from the Elizabethan still-room stuff and the keeping quiet," said Jo-Ann.

"Apart from the skivvying and the fitting in and the shutting up," Willoughby said.

Edward held still and gave his mind to his wife. "You know, she's inventive, you see, and she has a much better brain than I have," he said at last. "She's a very subtle woman, not at all vulgar, and her intellectual instincts are probably as sound as anyone's I've known. I'd rather talk to her than to any other friend I've ever had. Of course, she's much more talented than I am. She has a beautiful sense of timing. Did you notice

when you were badgering her how she got interested in remembering Pempie and then could leave the room? She's always known how to get the action into her own corner at the
end of the round. It's like a great athlete. I once read about a
boxer who did that. She doesn't even think about it. I always
have to think about things. The boxer: the end of the round,
the bell went, his seconds had put down his stool, he was
there to sit, and his opponent had to walk the whole way back
to his own corner. I read about it in a book and it reminded
me of her. It was said that he learned it by practicing shad-
owboxing to popular tunes that ran exactly three minutes on
the gramophone. He got the rhythm into the back of his mind
somewhere. She'll be here in a moment. Do you mind not
pressing her about the drowning? I nearly lost her, you know.
She didn't breathe for a long time. May we talk about something else?"

Emily came into the room with an ice bucket.

Maximilian said, "The law has influenced you very much,
hasn't it? And your plays and radio programs have influenced
Sir Edward."

"I've picked up a bit," Emily said, "but the law takes a kind
of mind. Sense of history. When to move. I haven't got that.
It's like an athlete."

"Why did you bring up *stare decisis* in front of me?" Willoughby said sharply.

"Don't be jealous, my love," said Emily to him.

" 'My love'!" Edward said, and she looked at him, and then
back to Willoughby.

"I brought it up because this is where I am. Decided
matters." She pointed unconsciously at her feet and the room,
meaning her life, and then moved the subject. "I don't mean
I've learned much about the law. I'd make a very poor show-

ing in a court. Do have a whisky, all of you. You remind me of a tribunal. It's like the time when I nearly drowned in the Mediterranean with you."

"You *remember* nearly drowning?" said Jo-Ann. "Sir Edward says you've got amnesia about it."

"Well, this does rather manage to bring it back," Emily said. "Archivists. It gives one quite a strong idea of what it's going to be like to be a corpse."

"A tribunal?" said Edward. "I'm sorry. Is that what it was like underwater? Was that because of living with me?"

"No, I should think it was because of nearly drowning. And anyway, it happens all the time. One's always in the dock and being questioned, isn't one? In one's mind. It's quite easy to accede to the charge that one's badly guilty."

"Guilty?" said Willoughby with hope.

"Of one's life."

"How do you account for being acquitted, then? For being here?" said Willoughby.

"Him, I expect," she said, looking at Edward. "That's the way I remember it. I believe that's what happened."

"Everyone said you couldn't make it," Jo-Ann said. "Everyone wanted to take Sir Edward away, because it looked as if you couldn't make it."

"He seemed finished himself," Maximilian said.

"You caught a breath or two and looked at him in the end," said Jo-Ann.

"They said he was going to die of exposure, at his age," said Maximilian.

"Willoughby tried, but he couldn't do anything much," Jo-Ann said.

"Nobody can do what he can't," Emily said. She gave everyone a drink. "Unless he has a terrific wish to," she said, coming last to Edward. "Then I expect he could."